County Council

cumbria.gov.uk/libraries

Library books and more......

24 hour Renewals 0303 333 1234

C.L. 18F

New York Times and *USA Today* best-selling author **Sharon Sala** has written more than eighty books that regularly hit the best-seller lists. She's a seven-time Romance Writers of America RITA® finalist, five-time winner of the National Reader's Choice Award, five-time winner of the Colorado Romance Writer's Award of Excellence, and has also won many other industry awards too numerous to mention. During that time, she has captured the hearts of countless readers.

She was born and raised in rural Oklahoma and still calls the state her home. Being with her family is her ultimate joy, and she finds great satisfaction in creating her stories, then sharing them with people worldwide who love to read.

Colleen Thompson lives in the Houston area with her husband, son, and the latest representatives in a string of rescue dogs that keep life interesting. Her books have been honoured with nominations for the RITA®, Daphne du Maurier, *Romantic Times Reviewers Choice*, and Dorothy Parker Award of Excellence, along with the Texas Gold Award and *Romantic Times* Top Picks.

A former teacher, Colleen enjoys hiking and observing wildlife, along with researching, writing, reading, and discussing her favorite obsession—books!—at every opportunity. She'll happily discuss them with you, too, if you'll contact her through her website at www.colleen-thompson.com, where you can also learn about her past, present, and future releases.

DEADLIER THAN THE MALE

BY
SHARON SALA
&
COLLEEN THOMPSON

MILLS & BOON

First published in Great Britain 2011
by Mills & Boon, an imprint of Harlequin (UK) Limited,
Eton House, 18-24 Paradise Road, Richmond, Surrey TW9 1SR

DEADLIER THAN THE MALE © Harlequin Books S.A. 2010

The Fiercest Heart © Sharon Sala 2010
Lethal Lessons © Colleen Thompson 2010

ISBN: 978 0 263 88551 4

46-0911

Harlequin (UK) policy is to use papers that are natural, renewable and
recyclable products and made from wood grown in sustainable forests. The
logging and manufacturing processes conform to the legal environmental
regulations of the country of origin.

Printed and bound in Spain
by Blackprint CPI, Barcelona

CONTENTS

THE FIERCEST HEART

BY
SHARON SALA

There's an old song that begins with the words, "You were my first love...and you'll be my last love." Every time I hear that song, I can't help but have a moment of regret for what passed me by.

First love is the sweetest, and the most intense. When someone is fortunate enough to have it also be their last love, they are truly blessed.

I am dedicating this story to all the lucky ones who never had to kiss a frog to find their prince.

"When the early Jesuit fathers preached to Hurons and
    Choctaws,
They prayed to be delivered from the vengeance of the
    squaws.
'Twas the women, not the warriors, turned those stark
    enthusiasts pale,
For the female of the species is more deadly than the
    male."
                    —Rudyard Kipling, *The Female of the Species*

Chapter 1

Stars Crossing, Kentucky
Ten years ago

Eighteen-year-old Haley Shore was teetering on a maturity milestone. Tonight she was graduating high school. Excitement abounded as her father drove into the high school parking lot. She kept moving from one side of the backseat to the other, scanning the scene to see what her classmates were wearing and how they'd done their hair.

Haley had left her dark hair loose, letting the length brush the shoulders of her sleeveless jade-green dress, and chosen instead to focus on her makeup. A little eye shadow to highlight her green, almond-shaped eyes, a cherry-red gloss on her lips and she was good to go.

Her mother had spent the better part of Haley's life criticizing everything about her, especially her height and her mouth. She was five-ten in her bare feet, with sensuously full lips that had been the bane of Haley's existence until

Angelina Jolie had burst onto the fame scene. At that point, Haley's attitude had shifted. Suddenly the face God gave her had become an asset, not a hindrance. While her mother continued to point out her flaws, Haley had grown old enough to realize Lena Shore was never going to approve of anything about her.

As her dad pulled in to a parking space, she leaned forward from the backseat of the car and tapped her mother on the shoulder.

"Mom. You brought the camera, right? Daddy...you have to get a picture of me with Retta after graduation."

Lena Shore frowned at the question as she stared around the high school parking lot, checking to see if Mack Brolin's red sports car was anywhere in sight. Even though she didn't see it, she knew it didn't mean he wasn't there. She wasn't stupid. The fact that she had refused to let her daughter date a Brolin didn't mean it wasn't happening.

"No. I didn't bring the camera," Lena said.

Haley's heart dropped. "Mom! It's my graduation! How could you forget something that important!"

"I just did," Lena snapped. "Get over it. There will be plenty of people taking pictures. Ask for a copy."

"You shot four rolls of film the night Stewart graduated," Haley muttered.

Lena's face flushed. There was no arguing with the truth, but she wasn't going to discuss the fact that her older child—and only son—was her favorite. Getting pregnant with Haley had been an accident, and she never let Haley forget it.

Ever the referee within his family, Judd Shore pulled into a parking space. "I'll go down to Kennedy's and get one of those disposable ones," he said.

But Haley's joy was gone. "Don't bother," she said. "Mom's right. There will be plenty of people taking pictures because they're excited, and proud of their kids who are graduating, even if you guys aren't."

Haley flew out of the backseat before her father could respond and stomped off toward the gym with her red mortarboard in her hand and the red gown over her arm.

Judd looked at his wife. In all their years of marriage, he'd never understood her. She made no attempt to hide her favoritism.

"You could at least have pretended you were sorry you forgot the damn camera," he said.

But Lena was too locked into her own thoughts to care what Judd Shore thought. She'd just seen Tom and Chloe Brolin pulling up a few cars over. The rage that she'd lived with for the past twenty years surged upward, flushing her face to a dark, angry red.

"What the hell are they doing here?" she muttered.

"Chloe's niece, Betty, is in Haley's class, remember?"

Lena's frown turned into an ugly grimace, but she didn't comment. Instead, she got out of the car, grabbed Judd's arm and walked into the gym with her head high and her eyes straight ahead.

Inside, Haley's hurt was already fading as she gathered with her classmates in the lobby of the gym, waiting for the signal that would indicate the processional was about to begin. Within the hour, she would be officially graduated, ready to go off to college in the fall.

She was ready to get out of her house on so many levels, she didn't know where to start. All she knew was that living on her own, however lonely, would be far better than living another year at home with Judd and Lena Shore.

Excited, she kept peeking through the doorway of the lobby, watching families filing into the gym, then climbing up the bleachers, trying to grab seats as close as possible to the makeshift stage the graduates would cross to receive their diplomas.

The second best part of Haley's night was that Mack would be here. Even though he was finishing up his second year of college, he was still living at home and wouldn't miss her graduation.

She scanned the crowd, wondering where her parents were going to sit. It was for damn sure it wouldn't be close to the front. Her mother made no bones about the fact that Haley's exodus to college was nothing to be sad about.

The only thing Haley had ever done that wound up on her mother's radar was fall for Mack Brolin. To say the Shores and Brolins did not get along was an understatement, even though no one ever talked about why. The few times Haley had asked, she'd gotten slapped for her trouble, and that had been that. Lena Shore might control her household and her husband, and even her son, but she could not control her only daughter. Haley was having none of it. Her mother and father's personal issues had nothing to do with her. She loved Mack, and he loved her.

The end. And after tonight…maybe a new beginning, as well.

Haley had always made sure there were plenty of opportunities for them to be together without her parents noticing. From the time she'd been old enough to date, Mack Brolin had been the first in line. And he hadn't needed to ask twice.

After tonight, everything about their relationship was going to change. They'd talked about it at length, and while Haley still felt unhappy about their decision, she knew it was for the best.

With two years at the local college behind him, Mack's plans were in motion. After having led the small college football team to nationals twice—the second time to a championship—he'd caught the eye of several big-time college scouts. A couple of weeks ago he had received an offer from UCLA for a full-ride football scholarship for his last two years of college, and he'd accepted.

Haley's first thought on hearing the news had been, *I*

will die if he leaves. But that wasn't what she told him. She pretended excitement, knowing he couldn't and shouldn't turn it down. It meant everything to his family, not having to come up with the money to put him through the last two years of college, and now his future as a professional football player was looking brighter every day.

Haley knew her family would never agree to let her attend the same college, and so, for the next two years, their lives were going to take them farther apart than they'd ever been before.

She also knew that if it was meant to be, Mack would still love her no matter how much time passed. She might appear to be a fragile female, but she had a fierce heart. She wasn't afraid to fight for who she loved and what she wanted out of life—even if her strongest opponent was her own mother.

A few minutes later the band director stood, tapped the podium in front of him and then lifted his baton. On cue, the band started playing, and the fifty-seven graduating seniors of Boone High School began to march onto the gym floor to take their seats.

Haley took a deep breath, put a smile on her face, lifted her chin and moved into step—in alphabetical order, just as she had for the past thirteen years—right behind Charley Samuels. The moment she entered the gym, she started searching the crowd, but she was no longer looking for her family. She was looking for Mack.

Mack Brolin had driven into the school parking lot within seconds of the Shores. He watched Haley get out first, and he could tell by the way she was walking that she must have had another fight with her mom. It was hard for him to understand how a mother could be so cold toward her child, when his own mother was such a warm and loving person.

Still, he waited until Haley's family got out of their car and started toward the gymnasium before making his move. The parking lot was awash in families and graduating seniors in their red caps and gowns. He remembered vividly only two years earlier being where they were tonight—excited and at the same time a little anxious, knowing his whole life was ahead of him. He'd had so many dreams and aspirations, but everything he wanted included Haley Shore.

He couldn't remember a time when he hadn't loved her, but they'd made it official the night of her sixteenth birthday by making love in the backseat of his car.

He still considered it the highlight of his life. Despite every nightmare he'd ever heard about virgins and first times for girls being painful, Haley's experience had apparently been just the opposite. If she had suffered, she'd never said a word.

What she had done was laugh when it was over and ask to do it again. That was the moment that had sealed it for him. How could a guy go wrong with a girl that amazing? Everything he'd done since revolved around how to make their lives better.

Now, here he was, two years of college behind him and within weeks leaving for a bigger college on the other side of the country. Living in California would put him in virtual isolation from Haley for two long years. All this time he'd been waiting for her to grow up and catch up, and now they were about to be divided by time and space. It was hard to be elated about his college prospects without her at his side.

Oddly enough, it had been Haley who'd urged him to go. The joy in her voice had been evident the day they'd picnicked at Willow Lake. As he waited for the coast to clear so he could sneak into the gym, he thought of it again, as he had every day since it happened.

Willow Lake, just outside Stars Crossing, was a hot spot in the summer. But Mack and Haley had their special place that no one knew about: a tiny inlet between two heavily wooded areas that no one ever went to. And so he'd taken her there by boat, wanting everything to be perfect when he gave her the news about his scholarship....

"Today is gorgeous," Haley said, as Mack ran the boat aground and then helped her out.

"Just like you," Mack said, eyeing her long tan legs and slender body beneath the jean shorts and T-shirt she was wearing.

Haley grinned. "Are you angling for something besides a fish?"

Mack chuckled. He loved her sense of humor almost as much as he loved her.

"I wouldn't angle. I'd just come right out and say it, and you know it."

"Okay, okay. I was just teasing, anyway," Haley said. "Bring the food. I've got the blanket. I'm starving. Are you?"

"Always," he said softly, watching the sway of her hips as she walked ahead of him.

A few moments later they had the blanket spread out in "their spot"—a large open space beneath the overhanging limbs of a giant weeping willow. Haley sat cross-legged on the blanket, poking through the picnic basket as Mack dug through the small ice chest for cold drinks to go with their food.

Soon they were eating their way through subs and chips, and washing it all down with cold lemonade, but it didn't take long for her to realize he had something on his mind. And Haley, being Haley, didn't mince words.

"What's up, and don't say 'nothing,' because I know better than that."

Mack sighed, then wiped his hands on his jeans and put his leftover stuff back into the picnic basket. She knew him well enough to know that if he wasn't eating, it couldn't be good. She dumped her own leftovers back in the basket, as well, and then leaned forward.

"Talk to me," she said.

Mack took a deep breath, then almost smiled. "Part of it is good news. I've accepted an offer to play quarterback at UCLA for my last two years of college. It's a full-ride scholarship, so Mom and Dad are off the hook. I couldn't turn it down."

She surprised him then, throwing her arms around his neck and hugging him with all her might.

"Oh, Mack! That's fantastic! Why were you nervous to tell me?"

"Because it means two years away from you," he said.

"It'll be okay, Mack. You'll graduate from UCLA, probably get drafted into the NFL, which is something you've always wanted. And two years down the road, if you still want me, I'll be here."

"Want you? Are you crazy?" Mack muttered.

That was when he'd laid her down in the grass and, in the bright light of day, stripped them both naked and slid between her legs.

Mack paused only once to look down at the girl beneath him—at the spill of her long dark hair, her Angelina Jolie lips and the green fire in her eyes—and then he started moving.

Haley sighed as he filled her. She wrapped her legs around his waist and pulled him deeper without taking her gaze from his face. He knew she liked to watch his changing expressions as they made love, though what she saw in his square face, straight nose and wide-set blue eyes, he didn't know. Once, she had called him beautiful. His pleasure had been an instant turn-on for them both—just like the passion he could see on her face now.

The sun was warm on their bodies, even though they were shaded by the sweep of willow branches brushing the ground. Birds were chirping in nearby trees, as if spreading the word of their union. A turtle slid off a rock and into the water only yards away, but neither one of them heard or cared. Right now, it was all about the moment and the feeling, the rhythm of making love.

Moments turned into a minute, and then another, and another, when all of a sudden he sensed Haley's focus begin to shift and he knew she was about to lose control. That was all it took.

Suddenly he stiffened, then groaned.

Haley gasped, then closed her eyes as his thrusts became harder and faster, and arched upward to meet him as a gut-deep moan slipped out from between her lips.

It was all Mack had been waiting for. With one last heroic thrust, he came…showering his seed into her womb in a powerful and continuous burst, then collapsing on top of her, a sweating, quivering mass of muscle. He couldn't have moved at that moment if he'd tried.

"Haley, Haley…I love you, so much. So much. How am I going to live without this…without you…for the next two years?" Then he began to rain kisses all over her face.

It was then he heard the catch in her breath and knew she was crying.

"Haley, baby…please don't cry," he whispered.

Haley laughed, though he thought it didn't sound entirely convincing.

"I'm not crying," she said. "I'm just trying to breathe."

"Oh. Sorry," he said, and rolled so that his weight was no longer on top of her.

Haley hid her face against his chest and—

Suddenly a horn honked. Mack jumped, his daydreaming brought to an abrupt end. When he realized the Shores were no longer in sight, he got out of his car and started inside. Within seconds, people were stopping him and congratulating him on his news.

"Hey, hey, hey…look who's here! It's Mack! Heard your

news, son. We're wishing you all the best in L.A. Don't let all those pretty movie starlets turn your head now, you hear?"

Mack grinned. Milt and Patty House owned the local newspaper, and Mack's first job had been delivering papers for them.

"I'll sure try," Mack said, nodded to Mrs. House and kept on walking.

All the way into the gym, it was more of the same. Everyone wanted to congratulate the hometown boy who was making good, and he kept smiling and walking until he got inside, then paused long enough to locate where the Shore family was seated. He circled the end of the bleachers, then took a seat above them. That way, when Haley spotted him, and looked up and waved, her parents would think she was waving at them.

He didn't like the deception, but like Haley, he had lived his whole life under the cloud of their parents' feud. And he wasn't giving her up for anyone. The next two years were going to be hell; he was scared to death that once she got to college, she would find someone new and that would be that. She'd voiced the fear that he might do the same, and he'd laughed. He didn't have the words to explain how crazy that concept was to him. All he knew how to do was love her.

Stewart Shore hid in the shadows and watched. He wasn't quite six feet tall and blond, while Mack was tall and dark. He hated Mack Brolin—partly because he'd been raised that way, and partly because Mack was everything he wished he could be, including a hotshot athlete.

Stewart had been a good athlete, but not outstanding. He'd been a good student, but not valedictorian, like Mack. This fall, when he went back to college, he would be going back to the one in Bowling Green, not off to the other side of the country. And the fact that his own sister chose to defy their parents' wishes by sneaking around with Mack only added to his indignation. He'd heard the gossip. He knew Haley was planning to meet Mack after the ceremony tonight. If his parents knew about it, they would have a fit.

Haley entered the gym as if she were walking on air. She saw her mother's face only seconds after she saw Mack and realized he'd chosen to sit in direct alignment with them so she could wave, which she did. Amazingly, her mother actually smiled and waved back.

And then the seniors were seated and the ceremony began. Haley thought it was somehow very anticlimactic. Thirteen years had just been condensed to a prayer, a song and two five-minute speeches. When they began calling out names, she felt as if the room had become a vacuum. Sound faded, until everything was a faint echo and the loudest things she could hear as she walked across the stage to get her diploma were the whisper of her own breath and the thunder of her heartbeat in her ears.

Then it was over, and flashbulbs were going off everywhere. Just in case, she kept a permanent smile on her face. Suddenly the air was full of red caps and tassels, and she was jumping up and down and laughing. Charley Samuels grabbed her around the waist and hugged her hard.

"We did it, Haley. We did it!" he cried, and then danced off through the crowd, laughing all the way.

Haley's glance went straight to the bleachers. Her mom and dad were already standing and looking for a way to get out. She wouldn't let herself care that everyone else was meeting up with their parents for pictures. She didn't need a picture to remind her of how little they cared. That was already branded into her soul.

As for her, she was off to Retta's house. Retta's parents were throwing a graduation party, and Haley had a twelve-o'clock curfew. She intended to say hi to everyone, then ditch the party and spend every spare moment she had tonight with Mack.

* * *

They were on their way out to the bluff. It was where everyone went to make out, and Haley wanted Mack's arms around her so bad that she ached. He drove with the windows down and the radio blasting. Her hair was whipping around her face and eyes like crazy, which for some reason made everything funny.

She was laughing at something Mack said when they suddenly realized there was a car coming up behind them, and coming fast.

"What the hell?" Mack muttered, as he glanced up into the rearview mirror.

Haley frowned as she turned to look. Even though she couldn't see anything but headlights, all of a sudden she knew.

"That's Stewart!" she cried, and grabbed Mack's arm. "I swear to God, that's Stewart."

"Damn," Mack said. "Couldn't we have this one last night without drama?"

"Maybe he'll go around," Haley said.

No sooner had the words come out of her mouth than Stewart began flicking his lights from dim to bright and back again, signaling for them to pull over.

Haley grabbed her cell phone and dialed Stewart's phone. He answered on the second ring.

"What the hell are you doing?" she screamed. "You're going to cause a wreck!"

"Tell that bastard to stop the car. Mom sent me after you, and I'm not going home without you."

"I'm not going home with you, and I don't care what Mom wants," Haley said, and hung up.

Mack frowned. "If you want to go home, I'll take you."

Before she could answer, Stewart rammed Mack's bumper.

"Son of a bitch!" Mack yelled, and fought to keep the car on the road. "He's crazy. He's going to get us all killed."

Mack started to slow down when Stewart hit them again.

Haley felt their car starting to skid, and then suddenly Stewart broadsided them. The shocked look on his face told her that he hadn't meant to do it, but when their car suddenly went sideways, he couldn't stop.

The sound was like an explosion, and then they were rolling and rolling and everything went black.

It was the hissing sound and the smell of burning rubber that woke Haley. Her head was hurting. She was upside-down, and couldn't remember where she was or how she'd gotten there. Then she heard a groan, turned her head to the left and saw Mack. Blood was dripping from his head and his arm and his leg, and she remembered.

Stewart! He'd hit them.

"Mack. *Mack.* You've got to wake up!" she cried, then realized his leg was pinned beneath the steering wheel and a mass of crumpled metal.

"Mack!" she screamed again, but he still didn't answer.

Her hands were shaking as she reached for the seat belt, and as she released herself, she dropped down with a thump, hitting her head and shoulder against the roof. After maneuvering herself around inside the confines of the crumpled car, she tried to release Mack's seat belt, but it wouldn't budge. He wasn't moving, and he wasn't answering her, and she was starting to panic. His leg was still caught, and the hiss of steam and smoke was getting worse.

The phone. She needed to find her phone to call for help. She'd dropped it back into her purse. But where was her purse?

"God, oh, God, oh, God, help me," Haley whispered, but it was nowhere in sight. It was then that she thought of her brother again. He'd hit them! He'd caused the wreck. Surely he wouldn't have driven away and left them. He would help.

She crawled out through a broken window and then dragged herself up to a standing position. Within seconds everything started spinning, and she dropped back to her knees, then rocked back on her heels and started screaming.

"Help! Help! Somebody help!"

But the night was silent and the road was dark, and there was no one coming to the rescue. Once more she pulled herself upright, and this time she steadied herself against a wheel until the world stopped spinning. When she finally walked out from behind the wreck, the first thing she saw was Stewart's car, smashed headfirst into a tree on the other side of the road.

"No, God, no," she moaned, and started running, stumbling, trying to get to her brother.

The windows of his car were all broken, and the passenger's side door had popped open. Haley crawled into the front seat and then fell onto her knees beside her brother. Blood was bubbling from the corner of his mouth, and coming out of his nose and ears.

"Stewart? Stewart! Can you hear me? Why in God's name did you do this?" she asked.

But like Mack, Stewart wasn't talking. In a panic, she backed out of the car, and as she did, she felt something beneath the palm of her hand.

Stewart's cell!

"Thank God," she said, and hit 9-1-1.

"Stars Crossing Police Department. How may I help you?"

"God...oh, God...I need help. We had a wreck. My brother and my boyfriend crashed their cars. They're hurt bad."

Suddenly the dispatcher was all business.

"Who is this?" she asked.

"Haley Shore. My brother, Stewart, and my boyfriend, Mack Brolin...they're both trapped in their cars. I can't get them out, and they're both bleeding. We're about two miles west of town on North Hollow Road."

"Stay on the line with me, Haley," the dispatcher said. "I'm going to send ambulances and the police. Don't hang up while I do that, okay?"

"Okay," Haley said, and then started to cry as she ran back across the road to Mack.

A few seconds later, the dispatcher was back on the line.

"Are you hurt, Haley?"

"I don't know.… I don't think so. I got out of the car on my own, and I'm walking."

"I want you to sit down," the dispatcher said. "You could have internal injuries. Just sit still and stay on the line with me. Help is on the way."

Haley sank to the ground right beside Mack's door, reached in the window and wrapped her hand around his wrist, then drew her knees up and lowered her head to keep from passing out.

"I'm here, Mack, I'm here," she mumbled. "Stay with me. Help is coming."

She was starting to crash from the adrenaline surge that had gotten her out of the wreck and across the road, and she could feel herself coming undone. Her voice began to shake, and when she started to talk, it came out in sobs.

"Haley…talk to me," the dispatcher said.

"You need to call my mom and dad," Haley said. "And Tom and Chloe Brolin. You need to tell them Mack and Stewart are hurt."

"We will, honey. Just sit tight. You'll hear the sirens any minute now. Can you hear them yet?"

In the distance, Haley could just make out the thin, high-pitched wail.

"Yes. I can hear them," she said.

"You're doing fine, Haley. You're doing fine. Help is on the way."

Chapter 2

When word of the wreck began spreading through Stars Crossing, it abruptly brought post-graduation parties to an end. The emergency room quickly became packed with Haley's classmates, who had come to be with her.

Judd and Lena Shore arrived within minutes of Tom and Chloe Brolin and their daughters, and the two couples sat on opposite sides of the waiting room, glaring at one another in stoic silence. Neither couple had spoken to Haley or bothered to ask after her welfare. The fact that she was mobile and alert was enough for them, even her own parents. They didn't seem to care that she was pale and shaking and covered in blood, or that she had three stitches in her hairline, bruises rising on the side of her face and kept breaking into sobs every time another friend called her name.

Her best friend, Retta, a short, perky blonde, was sitting with her, running interference every time someone asked too many questions for which Haley had no answers.

An outpouring of blood donations had come in from

friends and families alike, but the boys' conditions were as yet unknown.

It wasn't until Jack Bullard, the chief of police, arrived to speak to Haley that Judd and Lena got up from where they were sitting and moved toward her.

"Hey, Haley…how you doin', honey?" Chief Bullard asked.

She shrugged, her chin quivering too much to answer.

"I know this is a rough time for you, but do you think you can talk to me for a bit?"

She nodded

Bullard smiled, and then sat down in the seat beside her.

"I need to ask you some questions about the accident."

"Okay," Haley said, and swiped her hands across her face, wiping away tears and smoothing back the tangles of her hair.

Bullard waited until she seemed to settle, then said, "I need you to tell me, in your own words, what happened."

Suddenly Lena Shore pushed forward and started screaming. The rage in her voice was impossible to mistake.

"I'll tell you what happened!" she shrieked. "My slut of a daughter was sneaking around with a damned Brolin. If it wasn't for her, none of this would have happened."

The minute the Brolins heard their name being slurred, they were up in the chief's face and shouting back at Lena.

"There's nothing wrong with our son," Tom said. "Your daughter is the one who kept chasing after *him*."

Haley shuddered and covered her face with her hands. This nightmare just kept getting worse and worse.

Chief Bullard stood abruptly and put one hand on Tom Brolin's chest and the other on Judd Shore's before they came to blows.

"Shut up!" he yelled. "Both of you. I'm talking to Haley, and unless you were in one of those cars, I want you all to be quiet."

Judd cursed.

Tom puffed out his chest.

And in the middle of the melee, Haley slowly stood. Something inside of her had finally come unwound. After all these years, she'd had enough. Suddenly the room went quiet as all eyes turned to her. Her words were angry, her own rage evident as her hands curled into fists as she spoke.

"Just for the record, Mother, not once during the two years Mack and I have been seeing each other did I ever *sneak* anywhere. Just because you people have issues with one another, that didn't mean we did. I love Mack, and he loves me. I don't know what's wrong between you and the Brolins, and frankly, I don't care. You people have wasted eighteen years of my life acting like children. You can hate one another… and you can all hate me…if that's what's going to make you happy. I don't care anymore. I don't care about anything but knowing Stewart and Mack are okay. After that, you can all go to hell!"

Her mother's face had gone from pale to purple, her father's to a dark, angry red. The Brolins wouldn't look at her, and her classmates seemed to be in shock.

At that point, Haley turned around to face Chief Bullard.

"Mack and I were driving north out of town in his car. We were just listening to music and talking when lights appeared out of nowhere in the rearview mirror. All we knew was someone was coming up behind us too fast. When I thought I recognized Stewart's car, I called him on my cell phone to be sure. When he answered, he began screaming at us to stop, that Mom had sent him to get me. I told him Mom didn't run my life, and that we weren't stopping, and for him to go home."

Lena gasped, and before anyone could stop her, she lashed out and slapped Haley's face so hard her lip split.

Chief Bullard grabbed Lena, but it was too late. "Ma'am, if you do that again, I will arrest you for assault."

"She's my daughter. I can—"

Haley pushed herself into Lena's face. Her voice was soft, but her tone was hard and clipped.

"I'm of age, Mother, and that's the last time you'll ever lay a hand on me, so back off."

Lena reeled as if Haley had just slapped her back. The fury in her daughter's face was so virulent, she didn't know how to react.

Bullard decided to let the issue go. "Then what happened?" he prompted.

Haley turned her back on her mother as if she no longer existed.

"Instead of going home, Stewart accelerated even more and rammed Mack's bumper."

At that point the Brolins gasped and started shouting at Judd and Lena, blaming them for Stewart's actions.

Once again Chief Bullard was forced to intervene. Within seconds, he put out a call for two deputies. They quickly arrived, and with orders from Bullard were told to keep the families apart.

"Now. If I have to calm you people down one more time, I'll arrest the whole damn lot of you. Are we clear?"

They didn't answer and wouldn't look at him. Once again, he chose to ignore them.

"What did Mack do when his car was struck?" he asked Haley.

She shuddered, remembering their panic. "Mack managed to keep the car on the road. The trouble came when Stewart rammed us the second time, even harder. Mack's car started to skid sideways, and before he could straighten it out, Stewart hit our car on the driver's side. I don't think he meant to, but he was going too fast to stop. After that…we started rolling. I don't know how many times, because I blacked out. When I came to, we were upside-down and off the road, and Mack was unconscious and bleeding badly. I saw his leg was trapped and tried to get him out, but I couldn't. Then I couldn't find my phone to call for help. I managed to unbuckle my seat belt and get out. Then I saw Stewart's car. He'd hit a tree head-on. When I went to check on him, he was unconscious, too. I found his cell phone, and that's when I called for help."

Lena was sobbing loudly. Chloe was weeping without making a sound. Both men were glaring at Haley as if she'd grown horns.

"It's ironic. The bitch causing all the trouble is the only one not to get injured," Tom snapped.

Haley flinched but didn't acknowledge the insult, and then, before any more slurs could be cast, a surgeon suddenly came out of a doorway at the end of the hall and started toward them.

"Is the Brolin family here?" he asked.

Haley held her breath as Tom and Chloe and Mack's sisters crowded forward, all talking at once.

"Is he alive? How bad was it? Will he be able to walk?"

"Wait…wait…let me explain what we did," the doctor said. "First of all, he came through the surgery fine. We were able to stop the bleeding and save his leg. He'll walk just fine."

"Thank the Lord," Tom muttered.

"But his athletic career is over," the doctor added.

"No…no!" his mother screamed, and leaned against her husband. Tom Brolin glared at Haley, then reached for his wife.

The doctor began explaining the intricacies of the surgery, how many pins he'd had to put in the leg and the muscle damage, but Haley had phased out. All she could think was that Mack was going to hate her. UCLA wasn't going to happen. His plans for a career in the NFL had ended before they began.

She dropped into a chair and covered her face with her hands. She heard Retta's voice, but not what she was saying. All she could think was, *Why, God, why?*

Then she heard her mother cry out. When she looked up, another doctor had appeared in the crowd—the one who had operated on Stewart—and he was saying something to her parents.

"No!" Lena screamed, and dropped to her knees. "No, no! Not my beautiful boy! If someone had to die, why wasn't it Haley? I never wanted her. Why couldn't she have been the one to die?"

Everyone in the room gasped, then turned to stare at Haley. Even her classmates were stunned by Lena Shore's words.

Haley froze. God…oh, God, oh, God. Stewart? Dead?

Judd spun, and before anyone could stop him, he yanked Haley up by the arm and began beating her with his fists.

"Daddy! No, Daddy, no!" she screamed, then doubled over, trying to block his blows by covering her face with her arms.

When she dropped to the floor, he fell on top of her and began pummeling her with every ounce of strength he had in him.

It took both deputies to pull him off.

"Lena is right! If someone had to die, why wasn't it you?" he roared.

Haley crawled to her knees, then pulled herself up. Blood was pouring from her nose and mouth. She was too dazed by the assault to even answer.

Judd Shore was still cursing and crying as the deputies dragged him out of the hospital.

A nurse came to Haley's aid and led her away, leaving Chief Bullard to see that Lena Shore was taken home. All the way out the door she kept screaming at God, angry that he'd let Haley live and taken her boy instead.

Haley found herself back on a gurney. Her stitches had to be replaced, and another three added. By the time they took her to X-ray, one eye was nearly swollen shut, and it hurt to open her mouth. When they finally finished working on her, it was after midnight.

The doctor who had been stitching her up stepped back to eye his work.

"I think that takes care of it," he said. "Where's your family? I'll have the nurse tell them you're ready to go home."

Haley shook her head, slid off the gurney, paused a moment to steady herself, then headed toward the door.

"No, Miss Shore. You need to wait for your family," the doctor said.

"I don't have any," she muttered, putting a hand to her rib cage as if to hold back the pain, and walked away. But she wasn't leaving the hospital. Not until she'd seen Mack.

There was no one in the intensive care waiting room except the Brolins, who were taking turns going in to see their son.

When they looked up and saw Haley standing in the doorway, whatever anger they had left turned swiftly to shock. Her face was so swollen that, had she not still been wearing her graduation dress, they wouldn't have recognized her.

Still, she was the last person they wanted to talk to.

"You have no business here," Chloe Brolin said. "Go home, girl. Go home."

Even though it hurt to breathe, Haley wouldn't let them know how deeply she'd been wounded. She lifted her chin, defying them to deny her when she said, "I want to see Mack. I have to see him."

"Well, you're not going to, because he doesn't want to see you. Ever," Chloe snapped.

Haley reeled, the words shredding her soul.

"You're lying," she whispered.

"No. I'm not," Chloe said. "You need to go home where you belong."

Before Haley could stop them, tears suddenly welled and spilled down her cheeks.

"I don't have a home," she said. "The only place I ever belonged was with Mack."

Haley stared at the Brolins, eyeing Tom and Chloe until, ashamed, they looked away, then her gaze slid to Mack's sisters, Jenna and Carla.

"You people…what's wrong with you people?" Haley whispered, then she turned around and walked away.

It took her an hour to walk home. By the time she got there, it was almost 2:00 a.m. She got the spare key from the birdhouse and let herself in the back door.

She couldn't believe how this night had ended. This morning she'd been on top of the world, and less than twelve hours later, that world had been permanently shattered.

She paused in the kitchen, listening to the house. As she stood, she heard a slight pop as the water heater came on, followed by the hum of the refrigerator. There was a drip at the sink.

She shuddered and sighed.

Daddy never did turn the faucets far enough off.

The ache in her belly deepened. Daddy. He'd tried to kill her tonight. If it hadn't been for the police, he might never have stopped beating her.

She took off her shoes and started through the house. There was a light on beneath her parents' door as she passed it on her way down the hall. She didn't bother to stop. There was nothing left to say to either of them. The fact that her brother was dead didn't seem real, but she took no blame for it happening. He'd done it to himself, even after she'd begged him to stop.

When she got to her room, she stripped out of her dress and underwear, leaving everything in a pile in the floor as she went into the bathroom. A short while later, after having showered and washed the blood and glass from her hair, she dressed in an old pair of jeans and her softest T-shirt, then pulled a suitcase from the back of her closet.

Her face was expressionless as she began packing it with only the necessities, trying not to think of the things she was leaving behind: toys she'd saved from her childhood; her grandmother's wedding dress, which had been bequeathed to her; all the things she'd been saving for her own home that were stored in her hope chest.

She didn't remember, until she was looking for ID, that her diploma was most likely lying somewhere along the highway, with her purse. She would stop by Chief Bullard's office in the morning to see if anyone had found it when they'd towed in the cars.

Finally there was no more room left in the bag or her small backpack. She sat down on the side of the bed, then stood again. She was in so much pain she knew she couldn't sleep. She downed a couple of painkillers, got her checkbook and the passbook to her savings account and added them to the rest of the stuff in the backpack.

Just before she started to close the bag, she remembered Mack's photo. She kept it taped to the back of her dresser mirror. She took it down, then removed a family photo from a frame on the wall and put Mack's photo in it instead.

Her heart was broken. Mack might not want anything to do with her anymore, but that didn't mean she didn't love him. She put the newly framed photo inside her backpack and slung it over her shoulders, then wheeled the suitcase out of her room.

It made no sound on the carpeted hallway floor, and once she got to the kitchen, she picked it up and carried it the rest of the way out of the house. The last thing she wanted was to look at her parents again. As far as she was concerned, her entire family—not just Stewart—had died tonight.

Her car was still in the garage. It had been a present from her grandmother on her sixteenth birthday. The title was in her name, which was good, because she was taking it with her.

She tossed her things into the trunk, then backed out of the garage and drove away without once looking back.

When the bank opened at 9:00 a.m. the next morning, Haley was waiting at the door. She'd already been to the police department, and recovered her purse and diploma. Chief Bullard had been kind and gentle, asking if she wanted to press charges against her father, which she promptly refused.

She'd walked out of the department with a hand to her midsection. The more time passed, the stiffer and sorer she became. She knew what she looked like: as if she'd been through a wreck, which she had, and beaten to a pulp, which she also had. She felt shattered in every way that mattered, but she still had her pride.

She passed through the bank lobby without looking to her right or her left, and walked straight up to the first teller she saw.

"I want to withdraw my savings," she said, and put her passbook on the counter. "I'll take fifteen hundred dollars in cash, and the rest in traveler's checks."

Stars Crossing was a small town. Everyone knew everyone else's business. They knew her brother had died in a wreck last night, and that Mack Brolin's athletic career had come to an end in the same wreck. And they also knew the only common denominator between them was the girl at the window.

They also knew that her father had been arrested for assaulting her, and that her mother wished her dead.

The teller's heart ached for Haley, but there was nothing to be said.

"Do you want that fifteen hundred dollars in big bills?" she asked.

Haley thought about it for a moment, then said, "All of it in hundreds except for four hundred dollars. I'll take that in twenties."

"I'll have to get an okay to—"

Haley stiffened, and then her voice rose. "An okay for what? It's my money! I've spent the past seven summers of my life working for it. It's in my name, and my name only, and I'm of age. You don't need anyone's permission except mine to hand it over."

The bank president heard the commotion and hurried to the window to put out the fire.

"Do as she asks," he told the teller, and then gently laid a hand on Haley's shoulder. "We're so sorry for your loss," he said softly.

Haley nodded.

Twenty minutes later, she was in her car and heading out of Stars Crossing.

She never looked back.

Chapter 3

"Easy now, Mr. Wyatt… Let me move your leg for you, okay?"

"'Kay, Ha-ley. I kee for-geh you in sharge."

Haley grinned at the elderly gentleman on her exercise table, proud of how far he'd come since the stroke he'd suffered six months earlier. His first trip to therapy he'd been unable to speak, and the entire right side of his body had been paralyzed. Now he smiled and spoke, albeit a little slowly and not always with perfect clarity, and he was making good progress on regaining mobility, however limited.

Her entire life revolved around her patients, and when she wasn't at the physical therapy facility where she was employed, she was usually making house calls.

She rarely thought about her life before Dallas, and when

she did, it was only briefly. Even now, after ten long years, the pain of what she'd lost was brutally real.

A short while later, a timer went off and Haley eased Mr. Wyatt's withered leg down slowly, then helped him sit up.

"That's it for today. How do you feel?"

"Re-dy ta dans."

"Dance? Wow! Then I'd better warn Millie to shine up her dancing shoes."

The old man laughed. Millie lived at the same nursing home as he did, and he'd informed Haley months ago that Millie was his girl.

Haley marveled that at their age they were still optimistic enough to want a romance. She'd decided long ago that relationships weren't worth the effort it took to keep them alive and thrown herself into her job instead.

She helped Mr. Wyatt into his wheelchair, then pushed him back to the lobby, where a driver was waiting to take him back to the nursing home.

"Here you go," she said. "Do your exercises like I showed you. Stay out of trouble, and I'll see you again in about a week, okay?"

The old man grinned and winked, and then he was gone.

Haley glanced at the clock as she turned back around, and then frowned. Where had the afternoon gone? It was already quitting time.

She moved to the employee lounge, clocked out, gathered up her things and then, with a casual wave to another employee on her way out, she was gone.

Haley had decided years ago that Dallas traffic at five o'clock in the afternoon was, most surely, the road to the ninth gate of hell.

By the time she pulled up to her apartment building and parked, it was dark. She paused inside the car long enough to ensure that the path to the apartment building appeared safe, and then she got out.

The air was cold and felt damp, like it might snow. She pulled her coat collar up around her neck as she started toward the front door—her long legs making short work of the distance.

Once inside, she nodded to the security guard.

"Hi, Marsh…how's it going?"

Marshall French, a widower from Austin, had retired twice, but at sixty-seven, had been bored staying at home and had taken this job for something to do. He admired this tall, elegant woman with green eyes and thick, dark hair, but he didn't know anything more about her now than he had the day he'd taken this job two years earlier.

"Fine, just fine," he said, then handed her her mail. "Have a nice evening."

"You too," Haley said, then put the mail under her arm and walked into the elevator without looking back.

She chose the seventh floor, then leaned against the elevator wall as the car began to move silently upward. Once the door opened, she took a right and within ten steps was at her door. She thrust her key in the lock almost without looking and, once inside, turned and locked the door behind her—turning all three locks before she even took off her coat.

She never felt safe. Not since the night when the world had abandoned her. Even though she had no reason to fear living alone, she did. The three locks were her security blanket, and she wasn't ashamed to admit it.

It was the sound of those three metallic clicks that signaled safe haven for Haley. She hung her coat in the hall closet, dumped her bag and keys on the table, then scanned her assortment of mail.

There were a half dozen envelopes and a couple of magazines—*Taste of Home* and her favorite, *Southern Living*. She tossed everything on the kitchen counter as she passed through on her way to her room. She did nothing at home until she'd shed her scrubs and showered. It was a mental "putting aside" of her professional self so she could relax.

Afterward, dressed in old sweats and a long-sleeved tee, Haley was leafing through the rest of the mail as she poured Coke into a glass full of ice when she noticed the postmark on a legal-size envelope.

Stars Crossing, Kentucky.

At that point, she froze. Coke slopped over the top of the glass and onto the counter, bringing her back to reality. By the time she'd cleaned up the mess, she had braced herself to open the envelope.

All she knew was, whatever it said—whoever it was from—it couldn't be good.

Your father is dead.

Haley staggered, then braced herself against the cabinets, shocked that she felt any kind of emotion at the news. What was left of her family had been dead to her for so long that she hardly ever thought about what had come before Dallas— except for Mack. No matter how hard she'd tried, he still haunted her dreams. Her response to this news had taken her completely by surprise. She pulled herself together and looked back at the letter.

His funeral service will be held Saturday, November 13, at 3:00 p.m., with a family/friends supper afterward at the First Baptist Church.

"That's tomorrow. Pretty obvious I'm not wanted if they waited this long to let me know," Haley muttered, then took a deep, shuddering breath, tossed the letter down on the counter and walked away. Her heart was racing, her thoughts tumbling from one scenario to another.

Why now—after all these years—would her mother even

bother? Assuming it even was her mother who'd sent the impersonally typed and unsigned letter.

After her first year in Dallas, Haley had been the one to wave the white flag by sending her parents a quick note, telling them where she was and what she was doing. She stuffed it into an envelope and mailed it at the same time she mailed her weekly letter to Mack. He never answered, but for a while she'd thought her mother might. She waited for a reply for almost a month, then accepted the fact that no one cared and never wrote again. A year later she gave in to the inevitable and stopped writing to Mack, too.

A few minutes later Haley returned to the kitchen. The letter was still on the cabinet—like a bomb, waiting to detonate. If she went back, what wounds would she open? She'd spent years building a wall around her heart. She didn't want to feel, didn't want to hope—didn't want to care—like that ever again.

"I'll sleep on it," she said aloud, then fixed herself some supper, did some chores, paid a few bills and finally did an hour of Pilates just because she was afraid to go to bed and close her eyes. She didn't want to remember.

But maybe this would be the way to end the bitterness she still lived with. Maybe going back would be what she needed to move forward with her life, rather than the imposed lockdown in which she'd been existing.

It was after 10:00 p.m. when she finally went to bed, and, as usual, Mack Brolin came calling in her sleep.

Haley was standing beside an immense body of water. When she turned to get her bearings, she saw a large weeping willow, with low-hanging limbs that swept the ground. The place looked familiar, but it took her a few moments to realize it was where she and Mack used to go to make love.

As she watched, the branches parted and Mack stepped out, waving for her to come closer. She tried to move, but her legs wouldn't work. He kept urging her—begging her to come—but she couldn't seem to move. And then Mack's image began to fade, which increased her anxiety even more. Just before he disappeared from sight, she heard him call out, "Go home."

And then he was gone.

Haley woke up with a start, her heart pounding, her body bathed in sweat, even though the room was cool. She threw back the covers, then glanced at the clock as she sat up. Just before midnight. The dream had been weird, but it solidified her next move.

"What the hell could it hurt?" she asked herself, then got up, pausing in the hallway long enough to turn up the heat before heading for the kitchen.

Her steps were long, her stride purposeful—almost angry. She didn't want this, but it was here just the same. She started the coffeepot, then headed to the extra bedroom, got a suitcase from the closet and returned to her room.

By the time the apartment was warm enough to be comfortable, she was already dressed and packed. She emailed her employer that she was going home for her father's funeral, and to please reschedule her patients' appointments or give them to someone else.

She filled her to-go cup with hot, black coffee, then made herself a peanut butter and jelly sandwich, stuffed it into a Baggie and dropped it into her purse. If she didn't dawdle, she just might get back to Stars Crossing in time to see her father buried. It wasn't what she wanted to do—but there were lots of things in life that were unpleasant and still had to be done. This came under that heading.

Within minutes she was out the door and in the elevator. The night guard was asleep at the reception desk as she passed by. She didn't bother to speak and just kept on walking. Thirty minutes later, she was on the crosstown expressway, pushing past the speed limit with a lump in her throat and a knot in her belly. She wasn't sure if she was going back for the funeral or from a subconscious hope she would see Mack. Either way, the outcome was unlikely to be good.

Saturday dawned in Stars Crossing with a raw wind and a threat of rain. Not a good day for a funeral, although weather didn't really mean much on such occasions. There was never a good day for a funeral.

Lena Shore stared at herself in the mirror, practicing expressions. Once she'd been a pretty girl, but disappointments and grief had taken that away. Now her expression was most often either dissatisfied or grim. The frown lines between her eyebrows and at the corners of her eyes had long ago become permanent and deep.

While she'd been bound to Judd Shore by their marriage and her lies, that part of her life was finally over, and she wasn't going to pretend to herself that she was sad. Still, there was a certain cachet to being a widow, and she intended to use it to her best advantage. She smoothed her hands down the front of her dress, giving herself a mental pat on the back for giving in to impulse and buying this dress a couple of months ago. With Judd's bad heart, this day had always been a possibility. She would never have admitted to herself that she was planning for his funeral, but when the opportunity had presented itself last week, she had done nothing to stop Judd's fate.

She gave her hair a quick spray to hold the style in place. Although it was still thick and wavy, it was entirely gray now, and she'd chosen to pull it loosely away from her face and fasten it in a thick fall at the back of her neck. Sedate and somber was the mood of the day.

"That should do it," she said, then put down the hair spray, gave herself one last look in the full-length mirror and headed for the living room to get her coat.

* * *

Across town, Mack Brolin was pacing the living room floor of his childhood home, wondering if he was setting himself up for another heartbreak. His father had been dead ten years—dying from anaphylactic shock after being stung by a swarm of bees only days after Mack got out of the hospital. Mack was still wearing the cast from his wreck and dealing with the pain of losing Haley when they'd had to bury his father. At the time, it had felt as if he would never be happy again. With the passing of time, he'd come to accept what was. And then last month his mother had passed away in her sleep, and with that, except for his two older sisters, his last link with his childhood was over.

After the funeral, and at his sisters' request, he'd stayed on at the family home to ready the house for sale. He had been a successful building contractor for several years now, so the job had naturally fallen to him. Walls needed painting, carpet and appliances needed replacing, and as the days had passed, he'd found one thing after another that needed some TLC before the house would be fit to put on the market.

He'd called in a team from his company to do the rough work—replacing kitchen cabinets, countertops and the like—but he was doing the painting himself.

It was during the renovation that he'd found the letters from Haley in his mother's things, tied in a bundle with a faded yellow ribbon—unopened.

Everything from shock to disbelief had gone through his mind as he tore into the first one with shaking hands. By the time he had finished, he was crying. The last one, postmarked almost eight years ago, had ended on a sad, disappointed note. At that point Mack was so angry he couldn't think. All these years he'd been led to believe that she'd walked out—angry with him because Stewart had died and, after learning his athletic career was over, unwilling to tie herself to a loser.

After reading the letters, his first instinct had been to find her, but there was no way of knowing if she was still in Dallas, the city of the last postmark. Eight years was a long time. She could be anywhere—most likely married, with children, and happily living her life.

He felt sad and cheated, but didn't know what his next move should be. He could hardly confront the perpetrators of the lie, because they were both dead. Then he thought of his sisters. They were due to come by the next day to see how the renovations were coming, so he confronted them with the letters. When he learned they'd been a part of the lies, he'd exploded.

"You knew about these? You knew she still loved me, and yet you let Mom and Dad feed me that pack of lies?"

Jenna, his oldest sister, shrugged. "It wasn't our business to interfere."

Carla, who was only two years older than Mack, ducked her head. "I wanted to tell, but Mom threatened us with murder."

Mack was so furious he couldn't think. "Some family! You're no better than the Shores...lying because of that stupid feud."

Carla started to cry. "I'm sorry, Mack. But you didn't see what happened in the hospital the night of the wreck. We were all afraid to make the wrong move. It was hell in that waiting room, especially for Haley."

"Damn it, Carla, let it go," Jenna snapped. "It's old business."

Mack rounded on her and jammed a finger so close to her chest that she flinched, as if afraid he was going to hit her.

"Shut up or get out," he said softly.

Jenna shuddered, then sat.

Mack turned to Carla. "What happened to Haley?"

"Our parents were sitting on opposite sides of the room."

"I don't give a damn about where our parents were," Mack said. "Where was Haley? What happened to Haley?"

Carla looked down at the floor, hesitated, then met her brother's gaze.

"Her family didn't ask about her injuries, or sit with her or anything. She—"

"Was she hurt? Mom and Dad always said she walked away without a scratch."

"She had stitches and bruises, but from what she told Chief Bullard when he came to talk to her, it sounded to me as if she saved your life. She regained consciousness in the wreck and tried to get you free but couldn't, and then she couldn't find her phone. She crawled out, saw her brother's car on the other side of the road and went to see about him. He was unconscious, like you. She found his phone and called for help."

"Damn it!" Mack muttered. "I am so pissed I can't think straight. So, back to the hospital. What happened to Haley?"

"When they came to tell us you were okay and that you were going to live, we were so relieved, but then they told us you would never play sports again, and Mom and Dad lost it. They went off on Haley, blaming her, calling her names. Then another doctor came out and told the Shores that Stewart had died, and her parents flipped out. Her mother started screaming, and asking God why he'd taken Stewart and let Haley live. She kept saying she'd never wanted Haley, and that it was all her fault."

"God in heaven," Mack said, and shoved a hand through his hair in disbelief. "Poor Haley. I knew her family was screwy, but I had no idea—"

"Oh, that wasn't the worst," Carla said. "When her mother freaked out and started screaming, so did her father. He jumped on Haley and began beating her up…right in front of everybody. It took two deputies to pull him off her. They had to stitch her back up again, and I heard she had a broken nose and ribs, but that was just gossip. I don't know that for sure."

Mack stared at his sisters. Their faces were familiar, but he felt as if he was seeing them as they really were—and for the very first time.

"I'm sorry, Mack," Carla said.

Mack's gaze shifted to Jenna.

She glared back until she saw the tears on his cheeks. At that point she threw her hands over her face, as if she couldn't bear the sight.

"What happened after that? Did you see her again? Did she ask about me?" Mack asked.

Jenna flinched, then looked at her sister warningly.

Carla shook her head. "He knows this much. He may as well know the rest."

"What rest?" Mack snapped.

"Late that night she came to the waiting room outside intensive care and asked to see you. She looked terrible. Stitches everywhere… Her nose and lips were so swollen, her eyes were turning black… It was awful."

"Ah, God…I didn't remember that," Mack muttered.

"That's because Mom and Dad wouldn't let her. Mom told her you didn't want to see her and to go away, to go home." Then Carla's voice broke and she started to weep. "That's when she said she didn't have any home, and that the only place she'd ever belonged was with you."

Mack felt as if he'd been sucker punched. For the longest time, he couldn't think past that image.

And then Carla started to speak again.

"Mack, can you—"

He pointed to the door. "Get out. Both of you. I'll stay and fix the house like I promised, but when I'm through, I don't want to see either of you again."

Carla wailed and started toward him, her arms outstretched. "You mean never? You never want to see us again?"

Mack shook his head, then stopped her before she launched herself into his arms. "You're both strangers to me. I don't know either one of you, and the little I do know, right now I don't like."

Jenna jumped up from her seat, grabbed her purse and hurried out the door. Carla was still pleading and asking forgiveness when Mack shut the door in her face.

And that had been two weeks ago. At the moment they were persona non grata around the family home, and they knew it.

But after the revelations of that day, Mack became obsessed with finding Haley. He even searched "Haley Shore Dallas Texas" on Google just to see what came up.

There were quite a few hits, but nowhere did he find an address or phone for her, and only one link came with a photo attached to a newspaper article, and it was his Haley—shown as the physical therapist helping rehabilitate a member of the famous Dallas Cowboys football team.

After that, he'd stared at the grainy photo for hours, trying to find the girl he'd known in the tall, Amazonian beauty with long dark hair and a sensuous smile, then debating with himself as to what he should do.

The debate was still ongoing when Judd Shore died and gave him the answer. He marched down to the police station and confronted the chief.

Chief Bullard was ten years older than he'd been when Haley Shore disappeared from Stars Crossing, but he never had gotten over witnessing the beating her own father had given her the night Stewart Shore died. And because of that, when Mack Brolin marched into the police station asking for help in getting an updated address for Haley, he ignored police procedure and obliged.

"You know I'm not supposed to be doing this," Bullard said, as he handed over an address he'd obtained through the Texas Department of Public Safety.

Mack stuffed the address into his pocket before the chief changed his mind.

"You know I'm not gonna stalk her," he said. "But she deserves to know her old man died, even if he was a bastard."

Bullard nodded. "That thing between your families…what's it about, anyway?"

Mack shrugged. "I have no idea. None of us kids ever knew. We were just raised to shun one another, which, as you remember, turned into a recipe for disaster."

"That's for sure," Bullard said, then eyed Mack curiously. "So…you really never saw her again? I mean, after that night?"

Mack shook his head. "The last thing I remember about Haley Shore was that she was screaming as the car started to roll."

Bullard nodded. "Well, if she shows up, I hope this doesn't turn into another mess."

"Maybe that's what needs to happen," Mack said. "The only person still living who knows what the hell it's all about is her mother, Lena." Then he patted his pocket. "Thanks again for the address," he said, and headed out the door.

When Mack got home, and before he could change his mind, he sent her a letter with the information concerning her father's funeral. He had no way of knowing whether or not Lena and Haley had stayed in touch, but after what he'd learned, he would have bet on not.

He was counting on the fact that if she got the letter, she would most likely believe it was from her mother. He hated the deception, but it was the only way he could think of to see her without just showing up on her doorstep. He'd know, when he saw her—*if* he saw her—if she belonged to someone else. And if she didn't, he was going after her again, with just as much intent and passion as he had when they were kids. In Mack's heart, Haley Shore had belonged to him first, and he wanted her back.

But that had been days ago. He had no idea whether she'd received the letter, or if she was going to come.

Then he glanced at the clock. It was twenty minutes after two. Seating at the small church would be limited, and while neither Judd nor Lena had large extended families, enough people would show up that he needed to get there soon to get a seat.

With a reluctant look back at the bedroom he had yet to paint, he went to get his coat and keys. It was a damned cold day for a funeral, but he supposed Judd Shore would no longer be concerned with the weather. The man was most surely in a place where grudges no longer existed.

Mack ducked his head against the cold wind as he stepped off the porch and headed for his car, and moments later he was on his way to the church.

Haley arrived in Stars Crossing just before noon, cold and exhausted from the twelve-hour drive. She'd been somewhat disconcerted by how little things had changed but at the same time glad to find there were signs of growth, like the new motel where she'd chosen to stay.

Even though her mother had undoubtedly sent the letter, Haley was certain she didn't want to spend the night in the same house with her. And she certainly didn't want to show up at mealtime. The house was probably filled with extended family, and there was no way she was going to face her mother on her mother's home ground in the middle of a hostile army.

Once inside the motel room, she lay down on the bed, set

the alarm for two-thirty and then closed her eyes. It seemed like she had just fallen asleep when the alarm went off.

"Oh, Lord," she moaned, as her feet hit the floor.

With less than thirty minutes to dress and get to the church, she dug a makeup bag from her things, shook out the black dress she had packed, then went into the bathroom.

At first glance she looked like she felt—exhausted and sleep-deprived. However, she might have left Stars Crossing with her tail between her legs, but she wasn't coming back the same way. She'd grown up and, in the process, grown tougher. If people were going to talk about her—which she fully expected—she intended to look her best, and that black dress and the high heels she'd brought to go with it weren't going to hurt.

There was no need to pretend grief for her father's passing. Her grief had been spent years ago upon realizing that she just didn't matter to either of her parents.

But, on the off chance that Mack Brolin was anywhere inside that church, she wanted him to see her for who she was now—a strong and vital woman.

By choice, Mack was sitting at the back of the church. If Haley *did* show up, he needed time to get his emotions in order before facing her. There were so many things he wanted to say to her, not the least of which was, *I'm sorry.*

The family had just been seated, and the pastor was about to announce the first hymn, when the church doors opened, sending in a blast of cold air.

All eyes except the widow's turned as the door slammed shut, and the gasp that came afterward was so loud even Lena Shore turned to look.

The last thing she had expected to see on this day was the woman walking down the aisle. All Lena could think was, *How did Haley find out?*

* * *

Every stitch of clothing Haley was wearing had been chosen with one thing in mind: to show her miserable excuse for a family that not only was she fine, she was thriving.

She knew her height was to her advantage, and with the three-inch black heels she was wearing, she was more than six feet tall. Her long-sleeved black dress buttoned all the way up the front, coming to a halt at a V-neck that covered her shapely breasts—high enough not to be racy, but low enough to accentuate what she'd been blessed with.

The lanky girl Haley had been was now a woman grown, with the body to match. Her breasts accentuated a slim, well-toned body. She'd left her long, dark hair loose in a cascade of soft waves. The only splash of color was on her lips—those Angelina Jolie lips—which she'd painted fire-engine red.

She didn't look to the right or the left as she moved, because her gaze was fixed upon her mother, who had risen to her feet and was standing at the end of the aisle, as if daring her to come any closer.

From the look on her mother's face, Haley immediately knew that her appearance was a shock.

So it wasn't you who sent the letter. No matter. I'm here, anyway.

Lena was so shocked she couldn't move.

When Haley reached the pews where the family was sitting, no one moved over for her to sit. The old Haley would have turned tail and run. But not this one.

"Move over, Uncle Saul," she said shortly.

And despite the ripple of shock that went through her family, her mother's brother moved.

Haley sat without once looking at her mother again.

Dumbstruck as to what to do next, Lena had but one option. She turned around and resumed her own seat.

The preacher cleared his throat.

And the service began.

The moment people recognized Haley, they turned to look at Mack. He felt their stares but wasn't going to give them the satisfaction of knowing how dumbstruck he felt.

That grainy newspaper photo hadn't done her justice. His childhood sweetheart had turned into a knockout.

Even though it had been ten years—even though the woman who'd just walked down that aisle was as far removed from the girl he'd loved as she could be—he knew he'd done the right thing. No matter how this turned out, there were things he needed to say to Haley Shore.

Chapter 4

The funeral was a blur. At first Haley's heart had been beating so loudly that she hadn't heard a word the preacher said; then she began to realize that she could feel her mother's anger as if it was a living, breathing thing.

And Lena *was* seething, not only angry that Haley had shown up unannounced, but that the day was no longer about Lena the widow. It had turned into "the prodigal daughter returns."

Haley's first "welcome home" moment came when the congregation began moving down the aisle past the family, passing the casket to pay their respects on their way out the door. Someone squeezed her shoulder, then leaned down and kissed the side of her cheek.

"So sorry, honey," the woman said, and then quickly moved past.

Haley belatedly realized that it was Retta—obviously pregnant and with shorter hair, but once her best friend, just the same. By the time the church had emptied and the only ones left were the family, a good dozen of the congregation had paused to either give her a hug or a kiss, or shake her hand. When her mother suddenly turned and glared at her, Haley didn't even notice. Her eyes were blurred with unshed tears.

Then she heard the doors shut and realized they were giving the family some private time before removing the casket and taking it to the cemetery. She wasn't certain what was going to happen, but there was one thing she knew for sure: this time, she wasn't going to run.

Lena didn't even pretend to be polite. The moment there was no one left inside the sanctuary but the family, she stood and pointed at Haley.

"What do you think you're doing, coming back here now, looking like the slut you obviously are?"

Haley unfolded her long length from the pew and stepped out into the aisle. She glanced at her mother, then arched an eyebrow.

"Well, I obviously came to my father's funeral. As to how I look, the DNA came from you and Daddy, so if you don't like my looks, you have only yourselves to blame…Mommy dearest."

Lena was shocked. Where had that cold sarcasm come from? Finally she managed to sputter, "What are you doing here?"

Haley glanced at the others—her extended family of aunts, uncles and cousins, who'd always used her mother's behavior as a guide to how they should treat her, as well.

"Oddly enough, I got a letter informing me of the services. I assumed it was from you. My bad."

Then she picked up her purse, turned her back and started walking up the aisle toward the exit.

"Where are you going?" Lena screamed.

Haley paused, then stopped and turned around. "Why, Mother, I didn't think you cared."

Lena doubled up her fists and started toward Haley when Saul suddenly grabbed her by the arm and pulled her back.

"Let it go, Lena. This is neither the time nor the place."

Lena shrugged him off, but she couldn't stop her anger from boiling over.

"You have no business being here," she accused Haley. "You ran away before your brother was even buried. The brother *you* killed. You don't belong to this family anymore."

Haley sighed. "Mother, Mother, you sound like a broken record. As for Stewart's death…that responsibility falls on your head."

All the blood drained from Lena's face. Even the others began to mutter beneath their breath, thinking Haley had gone too far.

"That's not true. If you hadn't been with that damned Brolin—"

"No!" Haley said, interrupting her before she could finish. "*That's* not true. If you'd just let it go, Stewart would still be alive."

Lena reeled as if Haley had just dealt her a physical blow, then braced herself against a pew.

"What do you mean?"

"It's simple, really. Graduation night was going to be our goodbye to each other. Mack was going to California. I was going in the opposite direction. Our lives were moving apart. We had agreed to give ourselves two years to see what happened. If we still felt the same way afterward, then we'd see where it led." Haley shrugged. "But we didn't get the chance for that to play out, did we? You had to interfere, like you always did, trying to control everything and everyone with your crazy, mixed-up hate."

Lena shivered, imagining Stewart's ghost had just walked up behind her.

"I didn't know. You should have—"

"What? Confided in you…my dear, understanding mother who always had my best interests at heart? Give me a break. You showed your true colors the night Stewart died. My conception was an accident. You never wanted me and made damn sure…my whole life…that I knew it. No, Mother, you're the reason Stewart is dead. Not me."

Haley walked out of the church without looking back.

Lena moaned, then stumbled as she turned to face her family. She couldn't read their expressions but felt as if they were judging her, just the same. Drowning in guilt, she pushed past her brother, then staggered toward the casket.

The preacher, coming back in, in the wake of Haley's departure, saw her falter and rushed forward, but not in time to catch her. Lena Shore had just fainted.

Haley walked out of the church just as a peal of thunder rolled overhead.

Perfect. Heaven was going to unload. Might as well. No one else seemed inclined to cry.

She headed toward her car without looking up, anxious to get back to her motel and away from Stars Crossing as fast as she could go. As far as she was concerned, this had been a wasted trip. Her mother was still a nightmare, and Mack had been nowhere in sight.

She was unlocking her car door when she heard someone call her name. Before she had a chance to turn around, the first drops of rain began to fall. She jumped inside, quickly slamming the door, then started the engine and drove away without looking back. The way she was feeling right now, the last thing she wanted was to revisit old times.

It wasn't until she was back on Main Street and headed toward the motel that she realized someone was coming up fast behind her. She heard a horn honk, and then saw that the driver was flashing his headlights, obviously wanting her to stop. She tried to see who was driving, but the rain was coming down too hard, and she wasn't pulling over. The whole scenario was too reminiscent of her last ride with Mack, when Stewart had been following them. For all she knew, it was one of her crazy family, trying to get back at her for what she'd said to her mother. Unnerved, she kept on driving. When lightning flashed just off to her right, she flinched, then drove through a light as it was turning from yellow to red.

By the time she looked in the rearview mirror again, the street was clear. Whoever had been behind her had probably caught the red light. Good.

Moments later she took the turn into the motel parking lot and drove up as close to the outer stairs as she could get. She grabbed her umbrella and dropped her keys in her purse.

"Here goes nothing," she said, opening the door and popping the umbrella as she got out.

Rain was peppering her feet and legs as she made a run for the stairs. Even in heels, her long legs made short work of the distance.

As soon as she'd reached the sheltered walkway, she closed the umbrella and headed up the stairs.

She was digging her room key out of her purse when she realized someone was running up the stairs and calling out her name.

Suddenly she panicked. Her daddy had beaten her to within an inch of her life. She wasn't about to wait and see if one of her uncles was going for a repeat. Without waiting to see who appeared, she jammed the key in the lock and dashed inside. She tried to slam the door, but she was too late. It flew inward, narrowly missing her head.

In a panic, she ran backward, then froze as the silhouette of a very large man appeared in the doorway. Before she had time to panic, he spoke her name.

"Haley...it's me."

Even though she couldn't see his face, she knew that voice.

Mack.

She supposed it shouldn't have come as a surprise that his shoulders were wider and he was taller than she remembered. But why had he been chasing her? Was she about to get another dose of ten-year-old rage?

Mack had been watching the side door of the church where the family was supposed to exit when all of a sudden he saw Haley come out the front of the church and stride toward her car. From the set of her shoulders and tension in her body, he'd guessed that she and her mother had locked horns yet again.

He'd groaned. That was his fault.

"Haley! Wait!"

But at the same moment he'd called out, thunder had pealed, followed by the first drops of rain.

"Damn it," he'd muttered, and jumped in his car.

It was pretty obvious Haley wasn't going to the cemetery, and from the expression on her face, she sure as hell wasn't going to her mother's house afterward.

He sped out of the parking lot after her and almost caught up with her at a light, but she sailed through it on yellow and kept on going. Mack smiled grimly, thinking some things never changed. Haley had always driven fast.

The second the red light changed to green, he accelerated through the intersection. There were only two motels in Stars Crossing, and only one on this side of town, so that had to be where she was staying. Still, when he drove into the parking lot and saw her running for the stairs, he began to relax.

"Bingo," he said, and wheeled into the space beside her car. She was already on the second floor when he got to the stairs. "Haley! Haley! Wait up!" he yelled, and took the steps two at a time.

He turned the corner just as she opened her room door and started inside. He leaped forward and caught the door just before it shut in his face. But it ricocheted off the flat of his hand and swung inward with a thud. He didn't realize until he saw her face that he had scared her.

"Haley…it's me."

He saw her shudder, and then all the tension slid out of her at once. That beautiful mouth tilted up at the corners as she hit him with a perfect dose of Haley sarcasm.

"You could have knocked," she drawled.

"I'm sorry…I'm sorry…I didn't mean to scare you."

"Thought it might be some more of my family out to string me up."

He was still trying to come to terms with what had happened to her the night of the wreck. Just the thought of her father beating her like that set off every protective gene in his body.

"Over my dead body," he muttered.

The wind gusted suddenly, and even though he was standing beneath the shallow overhang, it blew rain down the back of his neck. He shivered.

"Can I come in?"

"Are you going to read me the riot act?"

"Hell, no. I have something to confess."

Haley frowned, then stepped back.

"So, come in…and shut the door. I'm freezing."

Mack stepped inside, then took off his coat and hung it on the knob, while Haley hung hers on the back of a chair.

"Sorry, it's dripping," he said.

She heard him, but her focus was on how he looked, not what he was saying. He was lean, but obviously strong. His arms and shoulders strained at the fabric of his white shirt, while his gray wool slacks clung damply to his long, muscular legs. From the way he'd moved, his injuries had obviously healed.

"Listen…" he began, then stopped.

Haley blinked. "I'm listening."

"I'm the one who sent you the letter."

Her eyes widened in surprise. "You? Why?"

He stepped back to his coat, pulled a packet out of an inside pocket and handed it to her.

"Because of these."

Haley gasped as she recognized the writing.

"My letters? I don't understand. I wrote those ten years ago. You didn't answer me then. What could you possibly have to say now?"

"My mother died last month."

Haley frowned. "I'm sorry," she said, and realized that she meant it. She remembered how close his family had been. "My condolences to your father, but what does one have to do with the other?"

It was Mack's turn to be surprised. "Haley, Dad's been dead ten years. He died the week after you left."

Haley was shocked. "I didn't know. I'm so sorry.… But I still don't understand what those letters have to do—"

"I'm a building contractor. I'm redoing the family home so we can sell it. I never saw these letters before in my life until I found them in my mother's things. That was a little over a month ago. They were tied together with that yellow ribbon… unopened."

Haley gasped. "You mean you—"

"Never saw them? Never knew you'd written to me? Right. What I'd been told was that you were angry with me because your brother died. Then, when you found out I couldn't play football, they said you didn't want anything to do with a loser and left town."

Pain shot through her like a knife as she remembered that night in intensive care, begging his family to let her see him.

"That's a lie. They told me you didn't want anything to

do with me…that you blamed me for the loss of your athletic career."

"Son of a bitch," Mack muttered, then shook his head. "After I found the letters, I confronted my sisters, who finally told me the truth. After that, I wanted to find you, but it had been so long I was afraid you'd moved on." He looked down at her hands. Although they were without rings, that wasn't proof.

"Have you? Moved on?"

Haley swallowed past the knot in her throat.

"I have a career. I have friends. But nobody sleeps in my bed but me."

Mack groaned. He couldn't stand it any longer. Within seconds, he had her in his arms.

"I'm sorry, Haley, I'm so sorry. For everything that happened to you…for everything you went through alone. I didn't know. I swear to God, I didn't know."

Suddenly the tears spilled and ran over. The tenderness in his voice, coupled with the warmth and strength of his embrace, was too much to ignore.

Mack held her tight, trying not to let anger at what they'd lost impact the chance they had now. He cupped her face, leaned down and brushed his lips across her mouth, then across her cheeks, tasting tears.

"God…sweetheart…don't cry. Don't cry. You're killing me with these tears."

Haley inhaled on a shudder and looked up. Even though he was bigger and older, he was still her Mack. She didn't know what the future was going to hold, but this moment had been ten years overdue. "A lot of time has passed. Maybe too much. Are you married?"

He shook his head.

She stepped out of his arms, but instead of walking away, she began unbuttoning her dress. "I want this for me. It does not bind you to my future in any way. Okay?"

Mack's heart skipped a beat. It was his only hesitation. Within seconds, he'd pushed her hands aside and finished the job for her. In a single motion, the dress was off her shoulders and in an ebony puddle around her feet. He reached for her bra, then stopped, and for a long, silent moment looked his fill.

Haley couldn't stand it any longer. She stepped out of her panties, then reached behind her and unhooked her bra. When it all hit the floor with her dress, she exhaled softly. She was free—free of everything, including their past.

When Mack began stripping, Haley's heart started to flutter. Then she saw his leg and the long, puckered scar running from midthigh to well below his knee, and she was pierced by a sharp stab of regret for what he'd lost.

Mack knew what she was thinking.

"Don't," he growled, and picked her up in his arms and carried her to the bed.

Haley shivered. So long…so long since this had happened anywhere else but her dreams.

Mack slid into bed beside her, then buried his face against the curve of her neck, inhaling the scent of her perfume. Like the woman who wore it, it was bewitching.

"You smell good. You feel good. I feel like I'm dreaming," Mack whispered, and then began covering Haley's body in an onslaught of kisses until she was writhing beneath him in a fever of need.

When he finally rose over her, Haley's legs parted of their own accord. When he slid into her, hard as steel and fully erect, she whimpered. But it wasn't pain she felt. It was greed.

"More, Mack, more."

He went deeper.

Haley groaned.

"Harder…please, harder."

Suddenly her head was against the headboard as their

bodies ricocheted off each other like bullets off concrete. The sensation was crazy hot, and it still wasn't enough.

One minute rolled into two, then three, until spots began to dance behind Haley's eyelids. At that moment cognizance gave way to madness as her climax washed over her. Wave after wave of mind-numbing pleasure burst and flowed in honey-thick motion, spilling into every nerve and muscle in her body until she was weak, shaking and gasping for breath.

Mack held on until the very last moment, but when he felt her sweetness suddenly melt and spill all around him, he lost it. Her legs were around his waist, her hands locked around his neck. He was dying inside her, losing his sanity in heart-stopping increments, and he never wanted it to end.

Then she moaned, and everything inside him came undone. His body bucked. His mind went blank.

Ten years of longing and regret were wiped out between one breath and the next, leaving them spent and trembling in each other's arms.

Mack rolled, taking her with him. When she would have moved, he pushed deeper, keeping himself buried as far inside her as he could go.

"No," he whispered. "Not yet. I waited too many years to be here. Don't make me move."

Haley threaded her fingers through his thick, dark hair, then cupped the back of his head and pulled his cheek against the curve of her breast.

"I never could make you do anything," she said.

"That's not true," Mack said, and shifted until they were looking into each other's eyes.

"Exactly what was it I made you do?"

He brushed his mouth across her lips, kissing her softly.

"Fall in love," he whispered, and kissed the tip of her nose. "With you," said, and kissed one eyelid. "Over and over," he added, then kissed the other. "And over."

Haley sighed. Could they start over—right now, in this bed—and pretend the past ten years had never happened?

"What are you thinking?" Mack asked.

"I'm thinking about the ten years we lost," she said. "Can we really get them back?"

Mack shook his head, then propped himself up on one elbow and began tracing the shape of her mouth with the tip of his finger.

"No. I've already lost those years," he said. "What I want is the rest of your life. But I'm willing to take it slow, if that's what you need. All I ask is that you don't shut me out."

Haley's eyes suddenly welled. "The night of the accident, your mother told me to go home, that I didn't belong there at the hospital…with your people. I told her that I'd never had a home, and that the only place I ever belonged was with you."

Mack sighed. The poignancy of her words was a physical pain.

"I'm so sorry. I can't change what happened to you, but I can change your future…if you'll let me."

"I don't know. Maybe. Like I said…the only place I've ever belonged was with you."

When she wrapped her legs around his waist, he quickened inside her. The sensation was all the aphrodisiac he needed.

"Again?" he asked.

Haley looked up at him from beneath those dark, sultry lashes, and then she smiled.

"Again."

Chapter 5

Night had finally come, bringing the day from hell to an end, but Lena's troubles were far from over. Learning that Haley and Mack had been planning to part company the night of the accident had been shocking. She hadn't been able to get past "what if?" What if she hadn't reacted so angrily on the night Haley graduated? What if she hadn't sent Stewart out to bring her home? If she hadn't, he would still be alive. But in the end, it all boiled down to one irrefutable fact: if Tom Brolin had chosen her instead of Chloe, none of this would have had to happen at all.

She walked through the house, smoothing out a wrinkle in the carefully folded afghan lying over the arm of the sofa, straightening the drapes so that they were hanging in perfect folds, then fluffing the pillows on the sofa before stepping back to eye her handiwork.

Everything was perfect. Everything except her life. It was in so much chaos it was pulling her down with it. When she glanced at the clock, her first thought was that Judd was late coming home from the gas plant. And then she remembered. Judd wasn't ever coming home again. She'd made sure of that.

She clenched her jaw and strode out of the room. It was time to go to bed. Sticking to a routine was how she got from one day to the next. Just because she was now living alone, that did not mean she could become a slacker.

She took her shower, brushed and flossed her teeth, then smoothed night cream on her face and neck before putting on her gown. She wouldn't look at herself in the mirror. She was a widow. It no longer mattered what she looked like, so she could suit herself. But the truth was, she couldn't face herself and the damage she'd done.

She started to leave the bathroom, then reached for Judd's sleeping pills. He'd suffered from insomnia for years, and while she rarely had a problem, tonight she just wanted to go to sleep and forget. She popped a couple into her mouth and washed them down with water before crawling into bed. Within minutes she was asleep. And it was in sleep that her dreams turned to the past.

The E.R. was in chaos. In her dream, the Brolins and the Shores were in adjoining bays, watching the doctors working over their sons and praying for a miracle with every breath.

Stewart's injuries had been assessed and the family informed. He had severe blood loss, as well as traumatic head injuries. His prognosis wasn't good. They were already talking about transfusions and brain surgery, and Lena was in a panic. She'd kept her secret for more than twenty years, and now, in one night, it was all going to come down around her head. When she saw Tom Brolin step out from behind the curtain surrounding his son's bed and head for the bathroom, she made an excuse to Judd and followed.

Tom was at the urinal when the door opened behind him.

When he looked up and saw it was Lena, he nearly jumped out of his shoes, then cursed.

"Are you out of your mind? This is the men's restroom! Get out!"

Lena peered beneath the stalls, making sure they were alone, and then began to talk.

"The doctor said Stewart needs a transfusion."

Tom rolled his eyes and quickly zipped up his pants.

"That's not my problem," he said. "For God's sake, Lena, get out."

She grabbed him by the arm and spun him around. "That's where you're wrong," she hissed. "Stewart's blood type is AB negative. You have to donate."

Tom frowned. "Why is that my responsibility? Mack might—"

"Because Stewart is your son."

Tom's face went slack, and he grabbed on to the wall for support. She knew he was suddenly realizing the importance of what she'd said. AB negative, just like his.

"You're not serious?" he said.

"I wouldn't lie about something like that. Not…now. Not when it means his life."

"Why didn't you tell me?" he asked.

"Because you chose Chloe!" she cried. "You made love to me, and then you chose Chloe!"

"I'm sorry. I didn't—"

Lena slapped him, her face flushed in anger. "I don't need sorry. Not anymore. I need you to donate blood to save our son's life! That's what I need. And I need you to keep quiet about it or you'll regret it. I swear on my son's life, if he dies, I'll make you sorry."

Lena moaned in her sleep as her past sins continued to play out in a nightmarish rewind. Maybe if they'd actually had that conversation… Maybe…

When a car driving past her house suddenly backfired, she woke with a start. Her heart was pounding, her nightgown stuck to her damp, flushed skin.

Rattled by the dream, she sat up on the side of the bed and went to get a drink. It would be all right. This would all go away. Just like always, she'd taken care of the problem. But as she padded through the house, her gaze fell on the stack of sympathy cards the funeral director had sent home with her. Thank-you cards. She was going to have to send out thank-you cards for the flowers and the food.

Satisfied that she had a purpose for tomorrow, she got her drink and had started back to bed when she caught a glimpse of her reflection in a mirror on the other side of the room. From this distance, and in the dark, it looked like Haley. It was the first time she'd ever seen the resemblance between them, and she hated it. The rage that had been simmering came back to a boil. How could she have given birth to such a cold, heartless bitch? Why was it her burden to be saddled with such an ungrateful daughter?

She'd seen Mack at the church, but he hadn't shown up at the cemetery. It could have been nothing—after all, it had started to rain. Lots of people who might have planned to go to the cemetery had changed their minds and gone home after the service. Lena couldn't blame them.

But the fact that Haley had left early and then Mack disappeared made her suspicious. She couldn't control her daughter any more now than she'd been able to when she was young, but she would be damned before she would see them together again. It had been the cruelest of tricks that her daughter and Tom's son had been attached in a way she and Tom never were. That was too much to be borne. And even though she got back in bed, her night was restless. She kept drifting in and out of sleep, kept waking in fits and starts, thinking that Tom and Judd were both sitting at the foot of her bed, pointing their fingers at her accusingly.

* * *

Mack woke slowly, aware first of unfamiliar scents, then the fact that he wasn't alone in the bed. That was when he opened his eyes.

Haley was lying beside him, one hand tucked under her cheek, the other on his arm. Even asleep, she'd been unwilling to lose touch. He exhaled softly, then allowed himself to look his fill. He still couldn't believe this had happened. He'd spent so many years thinking she hadn't wanted him, and to find out she'd been told the same thing, that he hadn't wanted her, seemed incredible. They'd spent the night waking up and making love, then falling back to sleep in each other's arms. But last night had been about more than endless hot sex. Last night had been about healing broken hearts and wounded spirits.

When he saw her eyelids beginning to flutter, he knew she was waking up. He wasn't sure what she thought about making love in the morning, but he was about to find out. He propped himself up on one elbow and brushed a kiss across her lips, thinking he was going to wake her slowly. But when she suddenly reached out and cupped the back of his head and pulled him close again, he realized she'd been awake longer than he'd thought.

"Surely you didn't think you were going to get away with that one measly kiss?" she drawled.

He laughed out loud as he rolled on top of her, then slid his hands beneath her hips.

Her legs parted.

He slid inside.

Haley wrapped her legs around his waist. "Is that what you want?" she asked.

"I want everything you're willing to give me," Mack said.

"I make no promises, but take what you want," Haley whispered, then smiled a slow, secretive smile as Mack began to rock against her, pushing all her sexual buttons and turning the passion dial up to high.

More than an hour later, they were finally dressed and ready for breakfast.

"Are you ready to start tongues wagging?" Haley asked.

"What do you mean?" Mack asked, as they exited her room and headed down the stairs.

"Us showing up somewhere to eat breakfast together means we probably spent the night together, too."

"Well, we did," Mack said. "We're adults. We answer to no one but ourselves, and besides that, there's no one left to cause trouble about it."

"My mother," Haley said.

Mack shrugged. "Talk's cheap, and as soon as I finish Mom's house, I'm on my way back to Frankfort...hopefully with you."

Haley grinned. It was the first time he'd mentioned a future beyond this motel.

"Is that where your business is located?" she asked.

"The home office is there. I have three crews capable of working on three separate projects at once. Right now I have a crew in Savannah, a crew in Frankfort and a crew in Alabama."

Haley was thoughtful as he ushered her into his car. Once he got in, she fired another question.

"Were you angry...about your athletic career?"

Mack frowned, then took her hand and gave it a quick squeeze. "Honey, whatever I was at the time, it never had anything to do with you."

"But it was my brother who—"

Mack's expression darkened. "He nearly killed you, too. I don't forget that. Ever."

"Okay. Then that's that," she said. "Question number two. How did you go from athletics to construction?"

This time he grinned as they drove out of the parking lot. "Haley, honey, look at me. I'm six feet four inches…two hundred and thirty pounds of lean muscle mass, with two left feet and no skill in culinary arts. Which means…I used what God gave me, size and muscle. After I went back to college, I worked as an apprentice for one of Dad's old friends on a construction site. I was strong. It was good therapy for my leg, and I found out I liked the business. Even better, I was good at it. One thing led to another, and here I am. How about you? Why physical therapy?"

Haley never hesitated. She was as sure of her reason now as she had been the day she'd begun her training. It was her way of doing penance for what had happened. The bonus was that she'd turned out to like it.

"Because of what happened to you. And like you, I was good at it, and I found out I liked it."

Mack's heart swelled. Yet another reason to love the woman his girl had become.

"I know there must be a lot of people who are thankful for your choice."

Haley looked him squarely in the face, wanting to make sure she wasn't reading this situation wrong.

"Yes, there are, but I can do my job anywhere."

Mack's smile widened. "Is that your way of saying you're thinking about renewing our relationship?"

Haley knew she was jumping into dark water without knowing what was down below, but she trusted Mack. For her, it was enough.

"Yes, I'm thinking about it."

"Then I am one happy man," Mack said, and took the turn into the parking lot of Martha's Diner, parked and killed the engine. Then he leaned over and planted a kiss firmly on Haley's lips.

She sighed as he pulled away. "What was that for?" she asked, as her stomach did a flip-flop.

Mack took her hand, feeling the strength in the muscles and thinking of all the good she was doing with her life. "Just because I could. Now. Enough of that. I'm starving."

Haley grinned. "Insatiable man that you are."

"And don't you forget it," Mack drawled. "After we eat… what's your plan?"

She didn't falter in her decision. It was something that had to be done. "To confront my mother. I think we deserve to know what that feud was all about."

Mack frowned. He didn't want to think of her getting hurt all over again. "You sure you don't want to just let it go?"

"As long as my mother draws breath, we're going to be caught in the middle of her hate. I like to know who my enemies are and what direction they're coming from."

Mack's smile shifted. "I get what you mean. Okay…she's your mother, so it's your call. Now let's eat."

He grabbed her hand and they walked into the restaurant together.

It didn't take long for word to get back to Lena that Mack and Haley had shown up together for breakfast at Martha's Diner. She didn't need a map to know how that had come about, and thinking about what her daughter had been doing when she should have been in mourning made her sick with rage. It wasn't fair. It wasn't right. Haley should have to pay.

Even worse, Lena began to hear Stewart's voice, chiding her for her rash behavior, blaming her for sending him to his death. She knew it wasn't real, but she couldn't get his words out of her head. She tried mopping the floors to occupy her mind, but it didn't help. Both Tom and Judd kept walking in and out of the room, sometimes separately, sometimes together, but always leaving tracks all over her clean floors. She couldn't seem to get through to them that they were making her job more difficult.

"You're dead!" she insisted. "You're both dead. Go away and leave me alone!"

The day was cold but the sky was clear. Haley was comfortable in the choice she'd made to wear jeans and a white cable-knit sweater. Her dark navy peacoat brushed the backs of her knees as she walked up the steps to her mother's house and rang the bell. Mack had headed home to paint walls, and she was already anticipating their reunion later.

When she heard the steady sound of footsteps clacking across the hardwood floors, she left her fantasies behind and braced herself for the confrontation. She knew before she entered that everything inside would be in its place, dust-free and shining. Beautiful to look at, but cold and unwelcoming, just like the woman herself.

When the door swung inward, Haley saw the shock come and go on her mother's face. Then, to her surprise, Lena stepped back and motioned with her hand.

"Come in."

Haley entered before Lena changed her mind, then took off her coat and laid it on the back of a chair.

"Here, let me hang that up for you," Lena said.

"Don't bother," Haley said. "I won't be staying long."

Lena's eyes narrowed as she lifted her chin. "So…do you have time to sit, or is this going to be another hit and run?"

Haley grinned. "Why, Mother…that almost sounded like a joke. I don't think I ever knew you had a sense of humor."

Lena's lips narrowed as she clutched her hands in front of her stomach and faced the thorn in her side full-on.

"What do you want? Why are you here? If you came to pick a fight, I'm not in the mood."

Haley eyed her mother carefully, noting a muscle twitching near her left eye, then the way she kept clenching and unclenching her hands. She looked like a woman on the verge of coming undone, and, to Haley's surprise, she felt a spurt of empathy. Even though there was no love lost between them, she needed to remember that her mother had just lost her husband. Sympathy might be hard to come by, but she could at least manage a little understanding.

"Sorry. Didn't mean to be confrontational," Haley said. "I wanted to talk to you before I left, that's all."

"Oh. You're leaving?"

"Soon," Haley said, stifling a smirk at the relief she'd just heard in her mother's voice. She sat down in an overstuffed chair and waited until her mother took a seat on the sofa.

"So what is it that we need to talk about?" Lena said.

"Why were you and the Brolins always at odds?"

Lena stiffened. "That's none of your business."

Haley leaned forward, resting her elbows on her knees. "But, Mother…you made it my business. You made it everyone's business. There wasn't anything subtle about the hate between you people, just like there wasn't a thing wrong with Mack Brolin except his last name, and that wasn't right. I'm not a child anymore. I think, at the least, Mack and I deserve an explanation."

Lena's nostrils flared. She could feel the blood rising to her face, and as hard as she tried, she couldn't keep from raising her voice.

"Oh. So it's 'Mack and I' again, is it? I know you spent the night with him."

Haley rolled her eyes. "Good Lord, Mother. I'm twenty-eight years old. Mack is thirty. Neither one of us is married, and whether I slept with him or not has nothing to do with what I just asked you."

Lena stood abruptly. "I won't discuss my business. What's past is past, and that's where it's going to stay. You know how I feel, and yet you continue to rub your ugly behavior in my face."

Haley stood. "And that's where your sick mind immediately goes…calling what Mack and I feel for each other ugly. Well, guess what, Mother? There's a real possibility that he's going to wind up your son-in-law one of these days, whether you like it or not."

Lena shrieked, then covered her face with her hands. "No. No. I won't listen to this. Get out. Get out!"

Haley put on her coat and walked toward the door. "I'm leaving. But this isn't over. You nearly destroyed the both of us, and I want to know why. Whether you tell me or I find out from someone else doesn't matter. You're not in charge anymore. And just so you know…even though there was no love lost between Daddy and myself, I am truly sorry for your loss."

Haley closed the door behind her and was halfway down the steps when she heard her mother scream. The skin crawled on the back of her neck, but she kept on walking. Even after she'd gotten in her car and was driving away, she couldn't quit thinking of how crazy that scream had sounded. Suddenly she shivered, as if a ghost had popped up behind her. She couldn't help but glance up in the rearview mirror, just to make sure she was still alone.

"Lord. Just one day back and she's already making me crazy," she muttered, and took the turn onto Main Street.

She hadn't gone far when she saw Retta and her mother coming out of the pharmacy. When Retta saw her, she started waving madly, trying to get her to pull over.

Haley pulled in to the curb and got out, smiling. Retta was already squealing and holding her arms open for a hug. Retta's little belly was round with a baby and she was a good five inches shorter than Haley, but her welcome made Haley feel protected and loved in a way she rarely remembered.

"Hey, you," Haley said, as she patted Retta's belly. "I see congratulations are in order." Then she smiled at Retta's mother. "Hi, Mrs. Woodley. You look great. Ready to be a grandmother?"

Retta giggled. "This will be numbers two and three, thank you, so she's already had the pleasure. However, Mother is in as much shock as Billy about this pregnancy."

Haley laughed out loud. "You're having twins? Wow. How old is your first?"

"Four. Thank goodness he's in prekindergarten or I'd be losing my mind. He's Billy all over."

"Billy who?" Haley asked.

"Billy Tyler," Retta said, and then giggled again. "I know, I know. Don't say it. I know I couldn't stand him. But he changed, okay?"

Haley grinned. "I wasn't going to say a word."

"We're about to go have some tea. Come with us. We need to catch up," Retta said.

Suddenly it dawned on Haley that Retta's mother just might be someone who could answer some questions about her own mother.

"Yeah, sure…I've got a little time," Haley said. "But only if it's on me."

"Great," they both said, and led the way down the street to a small tearoom—another new addition to Stars Crossing.

"This is nice," Haley said, as they walked inside.

Mrs. Woodley nodded. "My cousin, Mollie, owns it. Let's sit over here, where it's quieter."

Retta giggled. "Mother, there's no one else in here."

Her mother grinned. "I know. But if it does get busy, then it's quieter over here."

Haley watched their byplay with regret, wishing she could have had such a warm relationship with her own mother, instead of the constant conflict with which she'd grown up.

As soon as they gave their orders to the waitress, Haley turned to Retta's mother.

"Mrs. Woodley…"

"Judy…call me Judy," the older woman said.

Haley smiled. "Okay…Judy. Do you mind if I ask you some questions?"

Judy looked a little surprised, but quickly agreed. "Not at all, although I thought you two girls would want to play catch-up."

Haley gave Retta's hand a squeeze. "She'll forgive me, just like she always did…especially when she hears the subject."

"What's the subject?" Retta asked.

Haley's smile disappeared. "My mother."

Retta rolled her eyes. "Oh. Lord. I am keeping my mouth shut now," she said, and held up her hands and leaned back in her chair.

"Judy, you grew up in Stars Crossing, didn't you?" Haley asked.

"Yes. Born and raised here. Never lived anywhere else, actually."

"So you've known the Shores and the Brolins all your life."

Judy nodded.

"So what's the deal between them?" Haley asked. "Mother just clams up and gets angry when I ask, and truthfully, after what their feud put me through, I would like to know what started it. Do you have any idea?"

Judy frowned. "You know…I never understood it myself."

Haley groaned. "Darn. I was hoping—"

"Well, what I mean was…when we were all in school, everyone was friends."

Haley's jaw dropped. "You're kidding."

"No. In fact, Lena had the biggest crush on Tommy Brolin forever. They were quite the item. Then Chloe's family moved to Stars Crossing, and Tommy never looked at another girl after Chloe."

Haley was so stunned she couldn't think what to say. Surely all that animosity didn't boil down to plain old unrequited love? People grew up and got over high school crushes, didn't they?

"Wow. I never knew that," Haley finally said.

Judy shrugged. "Tom married Chloe about a month after high school graduation. Your mom and Judd got married before them, but not by much."

"Good Lord," Haley muttered, and glanced at Retta. "Did you know this?"

"Shoot, no. If I had, you know I would have told you. I never could keep a secret." Then she giggled.

Haley smiled. "I never knew until just now, but I've been missing that giggle."

Retta's eyes teared. "Oh, honey...you're going to make me cry." She grabbed a paper napkin from the table dispenser, blew her nose, then giggled again. "Sorry. These days, everything makes me cry. So...changing the subject. Sorry about your dad."

"It might as well have been a stranger," Haley said.

Retta frowned. "You guys never made up? I mean...after the, uh, the thing at..."

"You mean when he beat me?" Haley said.

Retta sighed. "And you never minced words. Yes, I mean after that night in the E.R. You guys never spoke again?"

"I wrote a letter home about a year after I left. No one answered. Figured that was that."

"But you came back for the funeral," Retta said.

Judy frowned. "Retta! For goodness' sake, honey."

Retta waved her mother's criticism away. "Oh, Mother. This is Haley. She knows what I mean."

Haley nodded. "I get it. Why come back now, after ten years of silence? It's easy. I got a letter telling me about his death, and the time and date of the funeral. So I came."

"Oh. So your mother finally relented?" Judy asked.

Haley smiled slowly. "At the time, I thought so. But as it turns out, Mack sent the letter."

Retta squealed. "I saw him at the funeral. I was hoping you guys could at least, uh, you know… He's not attached or anything." Then her eyes widened. "Are *you?*"

"No," Haley said.

"Have you talked to him?" Retta asked.

Haley smiled. "Let's just say we got some issues settled between us and decided to see what happens next."

Retta leaned back and folded her hands across her round belly.

"You'll wind up together. I just know it. You two were meant to be together."

Haley shook her head. "Thank you, oh wise one, for the prediction."

They laughed again, and then their order arrived and the hour passed.

By the time they were ready to part company, Haley realized it was nearly noon.

"It's been great seeing you two again. Judy, thank you for the information. Retta, behave. I've gotta go or Mack will be wondering what happened to me."

"Be happy!" Retta said.

Haley nodded. "Doing my best."

By the time they exited the tearoom, the sky had turned overcast, making the day seem even colder than it had before.

Haley jumped in her car and headed across town to the Brolin house to see what Mack wanted for lunch.

Chapter 6

Haley parked behind Mack's car and made a dash toward the house. Mack met her at the door before she could knock, swept her up in his arms and then kicked the door shut.

One moment she was laughing and breathless, and the next he had her up against the wall and was kissing her senseless.

They were at the point of looking for a bedroom when Mack's phone began to ring.

"Darn it," he muttered, as he glanced at the caller ID. "I've got to take this. It's one of my foremen."

He pressed a finger against Haley's lips to seal their last kiss, then winked and walked away.

She couldn't help but stare at the wide sweep of his shoulders and the taut shape of his backside as he sauntered out of the room.

"Lord have mercy," she muttered. What a big man he'd turned out to be—a big man who made her ache for his touch. Where was her resolve to take this slow?

As she waited for Mack to finish the call, she began wandering through the rooms, trying to picture him growing up in this house and wondering how he felt about selling it. Unlike her, he'd had a wonderful childhood. There had to be lots of great memories in the place.

She paused in front of a grouping of photos in what she guessed was the den, then laughed out loud. There was a school picture of Mack from about second or third grade. His hair was sticking out on one side, and he was missing a tooth. But it was the grin that stole her heart. Even then, the little devil in his personality had been apparent.

As she started to move on, something crashed to the floor in another room. She heard a very loud thump, the sound of breaking glass and then curses. Her heart skipped a beat as she spun and started running.

"Mack! Mack! Where are you?" she yelled.

"In the kitchen!" he yelled back.

She took a right in the hall and burst into the room just as Mack moved from cabinet to sink. Blood was dripping steadily down his arm and onto the floor.

"Oh, no! What happened?" Haley cried, as she ran to his side.

"I was on that ladder, which is now on the floor, screwing on that new light fixture, which is also now on the floor, when it just fell apart in my hands. It must have been cracked already and I didn't see it."

As Haley unbuttoned his sleeve and shoved it up his arm for a better look, her stomach rolled.

"Mack, this is bad. That cut is almost to the muscle."

"What do you mean, almost?" he asked. "I'm the man, therefore it's all muscle."

"So you're bleeding like crazy and you still have to be macho?"

His grin was a little shaky, but it was definitely there.

"You're impossible," she said.

She yanked a dish towel from a nearby rack, tied it firmly above the cut, grabbed his coat from the back of a nearby chair and threw it over his shoulders.

"Come on," she said. "We're going to the E.R."

The fact that he didn't argue caused her even more concern.

By the time she got him in the car and jumped behind the wheel, her mind was racing.

"Is the hospital still in the same location?" she asked.

He nodded, then leaned back against the seat and closed his eyes.

She gunned the engine, backed out of the driveway and left rubber on the pavement as she drove away.

"I would like to get there in one piece, thank you," Mack grumbled.

"Too late. You already took care of that yourself," Haley fired back.

He winced as she took a curve on what felt like two wheels. "I predict at least one of our kids will love NASCAR."

"Shut up," Haley muttered, and then cursed beneath her breath as she glanced into the rearview mirror. "We've got company. Dang it!"

She pulled over to the side of the street as a police car pulled up behind her with lights flashing. Before the cop could get out, Haley was out and running toward the cruiser.

"Mack cut his arm badly. He's bleeding...."

Chief Jack Bullard hadn't seen Haley Shore in ten years. It looked like her...and yet it didn't.

"Haley?"

"Yes, it's me, Chief. Mack's hurt. Gotta get to the E.R."

"Good Lord, girl. You two are an accident just waiting to happen," he muttered. "Get back in your car and fall in behind me. I'll get you there."

Haley ran back and jumped in the car, and when the chief

pulled out in front of her with lights and sirens running, she put the car in gear.

"Hang on, honey," she said shortly. "We'll be there in no time."

Blood had already soaked through the dish towel and was running down his arm again. Haley groaned beneath her breath as she saw the blood, then accelerated, following the police cruiser all the way through Stars Crossing to the hospital. By the time they arrived, a doctor and two nurses were waiting outside with a gurney. Obviously the chief had radioed ahead.

Haley wheeled up under the drive-through and slammed the shift into Park. She was out and circling the car just as a nurse opened the door for Mack to get out.

Mack swung his legs out and was about to stand when Haley slid her arm around his waist and pulled him out. It was the first time he realized how strong she was, and how adept she must be at her job. As heavy as he was, she'd almost lifted him off the ground as she helped him onto the gurney.

"Lie back, son," the doctor said, and Mack stretched out as ordered.

Seconds later, they were pushing him inside.

"I've got to move the car, Mack, then I'll be right there."

She turned around just as Chief Bullard walked up.

"Thank you so much," she said, and threw her arms around his neck.

Bullard grinned. "You're welcome, honey." Then he saw the inside of her car and winced. "Damn, he must have cut a vein. What happened?"

"He was hanging a light fixture at his mother's house and said it just broke. I need to move the car and then get inside. Thanks again," she said, and jumped into her car.

"Slowly!" Bullard yelled.

Haley nodded, pulled out of the drive and into a nearby

parking place, then jumped out and dashed past him through the door.

They'd cut the sleeve off Mack's shirt and were cleaning out the wound when Haley flew into the cubicle.

"Make sure it didn't cut—"

"Honey, I'm okay," Mack said.

Haley sank against the wall as her legs began to shake. Now that his care was out of her hands, the adrenaline racing through her system was beginning to ebb, sending her crashing.

"Thank goodness," she said. "I'll just wait over there in that chair...out of the way."

She stumbled out of the cubicle and into the chair across the hall, and sat down with a thump. Someone came over and slid into the seat beside her.

"Hi, Haley. It's me, Myrna Fisher. I used to babysit you, do you remember?"

Haley looked at the nurse, then nodded. "Of course I remember you. How have you been?"

"About the same. Sorry about your father," she said.

Haley nodded.

"Mack's going to be okay," Myrna said, then patted Haley's arm. "I haven't seen you since the night of your graduation. I was on duty that night when they brought all you kids in."

Haley shuddered. Sitting like this in the E.R. had brought back all the bad memories. And then having Mrs. Fisher refer to it again just emphasized the unhappiness.

"I don't remember," Haley said.

"And no wonder," Myrna said. "That was a bad night. Both boys hurt so bad. You were the miracle of it all. We couldn't get over the fact that you'd walked in on your own steam when they were in such bad shape. You were blessed, honey...and meant to survive. You saved them."

"Not Stewart," Haley said. "Stewart died."

"But not from neglect. You did your part. The doctor who

operated was a genius. Everyone was donating blood to help. I remember the panic when we typed Stewart's blood and found out it was AB negative. That's pretty rare. Even though Mr. Brolin was a match and donated, it still didn't save him."

At first, it didn't sink it. And then suddenly, Haley sat up. "Mr. Brolin donated blood for my brother?"

"Yes."

"Not my dad. Not my mom. Mr. Brolin?"

Suddenly Myrna realized what she'd inadvertently revealed. Her face flushed, and she averted her gaze. "Oh. I'm so sorry. I don't know what I was thinking. Please…I shouldn't have—"

She jumped up and hurried away, but the damage had been done.

Haley's thoughts had gone into free fall. Her mother used to date Tom Brolin. Tom Brolin, not her dad, had the same blood type as Stewart.

"Oh. My. God."

Someone tapped Haley on the arm. "Mack's getting stitches now. He's asking for you."

Haley hurried back into the cubicle as they were deadening the area to be stitched. Mack was white-lipped and pale, but he managed a crooked smile when he saw her walk in.

"There's my girl," he said softly, and held out his hand.

She clutched it gratefully, then stood by his side, watching intently as the doctor took fifteen stitches to close the cut.

After a bandage, a prescription for pain relievers and a reminder to call for an appointment to have the stitches removed later, they were ready to go.

"I need to move the car up to the drive-through," Haley said, as an orderly went to get a wheelchair for Mack.

"Wait," he said, and then tugged at her hand.

She leaned over the bed and kissed him square on the mouth, groaning beneath her breath as she pulled back.

"You scared me," she said.

"Scared myself, too," Mack said, and then frowned at her. "You know what this means, don't you?"

Haley glanced at the bandage on his arm, then at his face. What had she missed while she was sitting outside? Her heartbeat skipped, then settled back into rhythm.

"What?"

"For a while, you're going to have to be the one on top."

Her eyes widened, and then she smirked.

"You're impossible, and I'm going to get the car. Don't do anything weird until I get back."

"Then we can be weird together?" he asked, with an overly innocent expression on his face.

Haley was still laughing as she went outside to get her car.

Lord, please let this work the second time around.

Lena was walking in circles. She had been for hours. One of her friends had called telling her she'd seen Haley having tea with Retta and Judy. She kept telling herself it meant nothing. That the little bitch was only seeing an old friend before leaving town. Lena wouldn't—couldn't—let herself believe that, after all these years and everything she'd done to keep her secret, it might be coming undone.

But she knew how headstrong Haley was. If she said she wanted answers, she wouldn't stop until she got them. Lena couldn't let that happen. She had a reputation to maintain. Good women didn't get pregnant without the sanctity of marriage. And then Stewart whispered in her ear. *Good women don't lie. Good women don't kill.*

She slapped her hands over her ears and turned frantically, screaming at a ghost only she could hear.

"Stop it, Stewart! Stop it! I didn't know! It wasn't my fault! She should have told me!"

She's going to tell. She's going to tell.

Lena screamed, then picked up a vase and threw it at

Stewart, but Stewart wasn't there, so the vase shattered against the wall.

She stared at the broken glass, then took a deep breath and went to get a broom.

"Waste not. Want not," she mumbled, and began to clean up the mess she'd made.

Haley took Mack back to her motel, rather than his house, and with a lot less fuss than when they'd left. He needed to sleep, she said, and his house smelled like fresh paint. Normally he would have opened the windows and let the place air until the scent was gone. But he didn't feel like any more discomfort, so he let Haley have her way. Besides, he liked being babied. It was a new and exciting prospect, being fussed over by the only woman he'd ever loved.

"Your shirt is a goner," Haley said, as she helped him pull the knit fabric over his head, then dropped the bloody now-one-sleeved garment onto the floor beside the bed.

"The pain pills are kicking in," he muttered. "My head is fuzzy."

"Your head is gorgeous," Haley said, as she pulled back the covers to her king-size bed, then unbuttoned his jeans and pulled them down to his knees. "Sit."

Mack didn't argue. "Are we making love?" he asked.

Haley snorted. "Eventually, but not right now. I do not intend for those stitches to pull out."

"But you could be on top, remember?" he argued.

She bent over and pulled off one of his boots, then the other, grinning as she worked. Then she pulled off his jeans and socks, and stood.

"You can lie back now, honey," she said.

Mack stretched out on the bed, wincing as he bumped his arm against the mattress, then closed his eyes and mumbled, "Have your way with me, woman. I'm ready."

It was the last thing he said before he passed out.

Haley covered him up, then picked up his jeans and boots, and carried them to her closet. She paused a moment to watch him sleep and was unprepared for the surge of emotion that swept through her. Tears blurred her vision as she quickly turned away. She was still having trouble grasping the fact that she was no longer alone in this world, and that, if she wanted, she was about to embark on a life with this man—this crazy, wonderful, hardheaded man.

She started to take off her own coat when the cell phone in her pocket bumped against her leg. She thought of what she'd learned. All it would take was a phone call and she would know for sure if it was the truth. Without taking time to talk herself out of acting, she took her room key and stepped outside to make one last call.

Lena was on her hands and knees on the kitchen floor with a toothbrush and a bucket of water, scrubbing at the grout lines in the white tiled floor. When the phone suddenly rang, it startled her. She started to let the answering machine pick up, and then she heard her daughter's voice and hurried to answer.

"Hello? Haley? Is that you?"

Haley frowned. Her mother sounded strange…almost frantic.

"Yes, it's me. Are you all right?"

Lena looked back at the floor. There were tracks all over it. How many times was she going to have to tell Judd and Tom to quit walking on her wet floors?

"I'm fine," she said, and swiped a piece of hair away from her face. "What do you want?"

"I just wanted to tell you…I know."

Lena's heart stopped. She drew a deep, shuddering breath as her heart finally kicked back in.

"Know what?"

"About Stewart…and Tom Brolin."

Lena's ears started buzzing. She shook her head and then put the phone back to her ear.

"There's nothing to know. I have no idea what you're talking about."

"You and Tom Brolin used to date in high school. You were a couple, right?"

"Shut up," Lena muttered, a strange light entering her eyes.

"The night of the wreck, Stewart needed a blood transfusion. Daddy's blood wasn't a match. Tom Brolin donated blood to try to save Stewart's life, but it didn't help."

"Stop talking," Lena said.

But Haley wouldn't stop. There were too many years of lies between them. The truth had to come out to set them both free.

"Mother, it's not the biggest deal in the world."

"I told you to stop talking. You never listen to me, do you, Haley? No matter what I say, you always do the opposite. I have never been able to trust you…even now."

She hung up the phone in Haley's ear.

It wasn't the abrupt click that bothered Haley as much as the odd, almost calm tone in her mother's voice. But the ice had been broken. Before she left Stars Crossing, she would try to talk to her again. They would never be friends, but she would like this war between them to be over.

Haley couldn't stop thinking about what she'd learned. When Mack woke up, she had to find a way to tell him, too. He deserved to know. She wondered if Stewart had known, and then guessed he hadn't. Knowing her mother, that was a secret Lena had intended to take to her grave—until the night of the wreck. Then she'd probably been forced to sneak away somehow to tell Tom Brolin. She doubted that he'd known before. As close as he was to his children, she couldn't imagine him denying his own son. Or maybe he'd never known. Maybe he'd just donated blood like everyone else had been doing that night.

Then it hit her. Had Daddy known? She would bet not. God, what a mess.

Mack woke in the middle of the night, needing to make a trip to the bathroom, trying to figure out why his arm hurt— and pretty sure he was dreaming, because Haley was asleep beside him. And then he remembered the events of the past thirty-six hours, his trip to the E.R. and the fact that he was coming down off pain pills, which explained his confusion.

As soon as he moved, Haley was awake.

"What do you need?" she asked.

"You," he said, and leaned over for a kiss.

She kissed him briefly, then threw back the covers and flew out of bed before coming around to help him up.

"Honey, it's my arm that hurts, not my legs," Mack said.

Haley blinked. "Oh. Yeah. Right. I guess I woke up in 'nurse mode.' Do you need any help?"

"I'm going to the bathroom. You can come if you want."

She rolled her eyes. "Yeah, you wish. Go do your thing. And bring back a glass of water. It's time to take your pills."

"Yes, ma'am."

Haley sat down on the side of the bed, shook two pills into her hand and then stared at the floor, unable to get her mother's story out of her head. For the first time in her life, she thought she understood what had made her mother tick. Shame. Everything that had set her off had been related to gossip or shame. Haley's shoulders slumped, as she wished she'd known all this years ago, but at the same time, wondering if it would have mattered. She still loved Mack Brolin with all her heart. Thank God it had been Stewart who'd been the cuckoo in the nest and not her. If she and Mack had turned out to be half brother and half sister, it would have killed them both.

She jumped as Mack appeared beside her.

"I didn't hear you coming."

"I noticed," he said, took the pills out of her hand and downed them, then chased them with the water he'd brought. "Yum," he said, as the last one went down. "I missed lunch… and dinner."

Haley focused. "I have food," she said, and got her carryall and dumped the junk food she'd picked up earlier out onto the bed. "Eat up."

Mack dug through the assortment, and chose a package of peanut butter crackers and a package of Twinkies. "Don't suppose you have a can of pop in there?"

"There's a pop machine at the end of the walkway," Haley said. "I've got change."

"Honey, I was kidding. Water is perfect. Don't go outside. It's too damn cold."

She stopped. "You're sure?"

"Hell, yes, I'm sure. What's the matter with you, anyway? I know you well enough to know something besides me is on your mind. Did you have another run-in with your mother?"

Haley sighed, then sat back down beside Mack, took the peanut butter crackers out of his hand, opened them for him and handed them back without thinking.

Mack smiled. She was something—still in nurse mode even when distracted.

"Thank you, baby," he said softly, and began to eat.

"I know why our parents were at war. I know why my mother hated your family."

"Really?" Mack asked, as he reached for another cracker, popped it in his mouth and started to chew. "Why?"

"My mom and your dad were once a couple in high school. Stewart was your half brother."

Mack choked, then coughed as he reached for the water.

Haley waited. She knew exactly how he felt.

"What the hell?" he asked, when he finally caught his breath. "How do you know? Are you sure?"

"The night of the wreck, your dad donated blood, trying to save Stewart's life."

"Honey, lots of people donated blood," Mack said. "You're just reaching for—"

"Stewart's blood type was AB negative. So was your dad's."

Mack froze. Holy shit.

"You're sure Judd wasn't also—"

"O negative…same as me."

"And your Mom?"

"O positive."

"Good God, Haley."

She looked at him and then sighed. "I know."

"How?" Then he grimaced. "I mean…I know how, but—"

"My mom and your dad used to date. They were quite the item in high school, until your mother moved to town. After that, it seems he only had eyes for her."

"Who told you that?" he asked.

"Judy. Retta's mom. I had tea with them this morning and started asking Judy questions. She told me all about their high school romance. Then today, when you were getting stitches, a nurse who used to babysit me started talking about the night of the wreck and let it slip about your dad's blood type. The minute she said it, she freaked and left, but it suddenly all made sense, you know?"

"Do you think your dad knew?" he asked.

"I'm pretty sure he didn't. He wasn't the type to be long-suffering."

"So now what?" he asked.

"Now nothing. I have an explanation I can live with. Even my dad was second best, and I…I was nothing at all. I feel sorry for my mom, but not enough to try to be buddy-buddy.

Besides, she's the kind of woman who's big on propriety. If she admitted that I'm right, she would never be able to sell her perfect persona anymore."

"Are you sad?"

"About what? Nothing has changed. Except us. And that would never make me sad." Then she smiled and leaned against him briefly. "Eat your Twinkies, Mr. Man. You need to lie back down."

"Aren't you going to open the package for me?" he asked.

Haley snorted. "Not if I have to be on top, too."

Mack grinned. "God, I am so going to love growing old with you."

Haley started to laugh and wound up crying. Mack looked horrified. She sighed, and took one of the Twinkies.

"It's not you. It's me. I've had too many shocks for one day…including the fact that you still want me."

She held up her Twinkie.

"I propose a toast. To us," she said, and tipped the end of her Twinkie against his, then took a bite.

Mack took a bite of his Twinkie, too, then kissed her. She tasted like sponge cake and sweet, sticky frosting. When he drew back, she sighed, then leaned against him and finished her snack.

Mack stuffed the last of his Twinkie in his mouth and then lay back down. Only this time, his eyes didn't close.

"Have your way with me," he said.

So she did.

Chapter 7

The past six days had been a godsend. Haley quit fighting her hesitation to commit to Mack, and gave in to going to Frankfort with him and trying on a new love affair for size. All that was holding them up now was trying to finish his mother's house.

She peeled the last bit of masking tape from the bedroom wall and then stuffed it in the trash bag.

"That's the last of the tape. Are we done?"

Mack nodded. "That's it. The house is finished, and none too soon. I need to be in Frankfort by day after tomorrow for sure. Have you emailed your boss yet?"

Haley grinned. "Yesterday. I am now officially unemployed. You're going to have to take care of me or I'll be homeless."

Suddenly there was a loud thud in another part of the house, followed by silence.

"What was that?" she asked.

Mack shrugged. "I'll check later. If it's a mess, I don't want to know."

Haley glanced over her shoulder. "I'll be glad to leave this town. All week, I kept thinking I was being followed. Too much paranoia for me."

Mack laughed. "You are so full of it. However, you will be glad to know that I have three extra bedrooms in my house. I'm sure one of them has a big enough bed for you, since mine is so small."

Haley frowned. "We don't need an extra bedroom. We just need a bigger bed in yours."

Mack laughed. "I lied. My bed is plenty big. I just wanted to mess with you."

Haley eyed the light dancing in his eyes. "I always heard you can never trust blue-eyed devils."

"You can trust me, blue eyes and all. I have references, I swear."

Before Haley could answer, her phone rang. She glanced at the caller ID. "I need to take this. We'll discuss your references later."

She walked out into the hall, talking as she went.

Mack couldn't quit smiling. She might be unemployed, but from the sound of her conversation, she was still concerned about the patients she was leaving behind.

He started a last walk-through of the house, mentally ticking off the jobs that had needed to be done before the house was put on the market. He'd just started in the back bedrooms when Haley caught up with him.

"Hey, there you are! Where's the nearest place I can fax some information?"

Mack frowned. "Probably the bank…oh, no! Wait. There's a print shop that went in about four years ago. It's behind the old Duvall Furniture Store building. You know…the one with the gargoyles."

"Oh, yes. Okay. I won't be long, but I need to send some detailed instructions to the therapist who's taking over one of my patients."

"Take your time," Mack said. "I'm just doing a walk-through of the house."

"No working without me," Haley said, pointing to his arm.

"I promise." He glanced at his watch. "It's already half past twelve. I'm starving. We'll go grab some lunch at Martha's Diner after you get back, okay?"

Haley nodded, blew him a kiss and then headed back the way she'd come.

Mack heard her footsteps as she ran through the house, then the slamming of the door. A few seconds later, he heard her car start, then a few seconds after that, she peeled out.

"Only Haley could lay rubber backing down a driveway," he muttered, then shook his head and continued moving through the rooms.

About fifteen minutes later, he'd gotten all the way through the house and was in the kitchen when he heard the front door open.

"I'm in the kitchen," he yelled. He listened as footsteps moved hesitantly closer. Thinking Haley might not have heard him, he called again. "I'm in here!"

A few seconds later, he heard footsteps at the door. He turned, the smile for her already on his face, and then he stopped, shocked by the woman standing in the doorway.

"Lena! I'm sorry. I didn't hear you knock," he said.

Lena Shore was standing in his mother's kitchen holding a plate of brownies. He didn't know whether to duck and run or ask her to sit down.

"I guess I didn't knock loudly enough," she said, waving the brownies for an explanation. "Where's Haley? I wanted to talk to the both of you together."

"She had an errand to run. She should be back anytime," Mack said, and then waved toward the kitchen table. "Please. Have a seat."

Lena sat the plate of brownies on the table and then removed her coat before sitting down.

"Those look amazing," Mack said. "Are those for us?"

Lena looked a little nervous, but smiled. "I thought Haley would be here, but yes, I brought them for the both of you." Then she straightened her shoulders and leveled her gaze directly at him. "I heard you were injured. Are you healing well?"

"Yes. Just a freak accident. Renovations are like that. Can I get you something to drink? There's juice, and I think there's still some coffee left from the last pot I made."

"No, no, I'm fine," Lena said, and then glanced over her shoulder. "Do you think she'll be long?"

Mack knew she was uncomfortable, and truthfully, so was he. But if this was the first step toward some kind of a reconciliation between Haley and her mom, he didn't want to mess it up.

"Those look amazing, and I'm starving." He had one in his hand and the first bite in his mouth before Lena could speak. "And they taste as good as they look. Thank you," he said, and sat down at the table across from her and finished the brownie while she watched.

"I heard you were getting the house ready to sell," Lena said.

"Yes. Neither of my sisters wants to live here, and I'm in Frankfort. Rather than rent it out, we thought it best to just sell it. It's a great house. Someone will enjoy living here. We sure did."

Lena smiled, but her mind was scattered. When Mack picked up another brownie and downed it in two bites, she frowned. This wasn't going quite like she'd planned, but what was done was done. There was no going back. Now if Haley would only get here, everything would surely work out. She picked at an imaginary spot on the polished oak table, then suddenly leaned forward.

"Did she tell you?"

Mack frowned as he swallowed the last bite of his second brownie, then dusted off his hands.

"Tell me what?"

"About Stewart. About your father."

Mack sighed. Damn it. Where in the hell was Haley when he needed her?

"Look. The past is the past. Let's just leave it at that, okay?"

Lena giggled. "She *did* tell you, didn't she?" Then she brushed a speck from the front of her dress and tucked a stray piece of hair back behind her ear. "She never could keep her mouth shut. I spent half her life telling her to be truthful and the other half telling her to shut up. She never could manage either one." She giggled again.

Mack frowned. Lena's giggle was weird and inappropriate, and what she was saying wasn't making much sense.

"Haley and I are planning to get married. You're the only parent either one of us has left. I know it would make her happy if you could be there."

Lena grabbed her purse, pulled out her compact and lipstick and applied a fresh layer of lipstick over what was already there. But her fingers were trembling and the lipstick smeared. She didn't even seem to notice.

"Have another brownie," she said.

Mack picked one up and took a bite, partly because he was at a loss as to what the hell was happening to her, and partly because if his mouth was full, he wouldn't have to talk. But when he was halfway through the third one, the room began to feel too hot.

"I need to get some air," he said, and started to get up, but when he did, the floor suddenly tilted toward him. "Whoa!" he said, and sat back down before he fell. "I'm not feeling so good."

The last thing he saw was the smirk on Lena's face.

* * *

Haley couldn't believe it. Her mother's car was sitting in Mack's driveway. She parked on the street and ran up the drive and into the house, calling Mack's name.

"We're in here!" Lena called.

Haley burst into the kitchen, her heart pounding, her eyes wide with disbelief. When she saw the plate of brownies on the table, she thought she was dreaming. And then she looked at Mack.

Something was wrong.

"Mack?"

He pointed at Lena. "Good brownies. Gonna eat 'nother inna minute." And then he laid his head down on the table and closed his eyes.

Haley gasped. If she didn't know better, she would think Mack was drunk. She turned on her mother. The gleam in Lena's eyes was almost scary.

"What did you do?" Haley cried.

Lena shrugged. "I did nothing. You're the one who couldn't keep her mouth shut. You should have minded Mother," she said in a singsong voice, and then got up and walked out of the kitchen.

Haley groaned. She grabbed a brownie, broke it in half and then smelled it. All she could smell was chocolate, but there was obviously something else in it. For whatever reason, Lena had intended to drug them. Haley put a finger on Mack's pulse. It was steady and strong. She hoped to God there wasn't poison in the brownies. Before she could call for an ambulance, her mother was back, carrying a tin of paint thinner.

Haley stared in disbelief as Lena began splashing it all over the floors and the walls, talking to herself as she went.

"Have to stop the gossip. You should have listened to your mother. Can't trust you. Can't trust anyone," Lena muttered.

Haley screamed. "Mother! For God's sake, stop!"

Lena turned and sloshed some of the thinner toward Haley,

who jumped back just in time to keep it from getting all over her clothes.

"I told Tom Brolin to save our son. I made him give blood, but it didn't work and he didn't care. So I made him pay. He's allergic to bee stings. Did you know that? I did." Then she giggled. "I turned a whole jar of them loose inside his truck. If Stewart couldn't live, Tom didn't deserve to live, either."

Haley gasped. She couldn't believe what she was hearing.

"You killed Mack's father?"

"I didn't do it. The bees did," Lena said, and then giggled wildly. "My hands are clean. My conscience is clean. Men are never happy with what they have. They're always wanting more."

Haley was sick to her stomach, and as scared as she'd ever been in her life. Not only had someone really been watching her all week, that someone was her own mother.

"I put up with Judd Shore as long as I could," Lena said, as she tossed the empty can aside. "People have to learn that I mean what I say."

Haley shuddered. "What do you mean…as long as you could? What else did you do? Did you do something to Daddy?"

Lena smoothed the hair back from her face with both hands, then brushed at the front of her dress.

"I didn't touch him," Lena said, then rolled her eyes and waggled her hands in the air. "I didn't touch him," she repeated. "He told me I was a cold, calculating bitch. I told him he was useless, and that the only child he managed to sire was a worthless girl."

Haley gasped. "You told Daddy that Stewart wasn't his? When did you do that?"

Lena spun, her finger pointed straight at Haley's chest. "Right before he dropped dead on the living room floor."

Haley gasped, then covered her mouth with both hands to keep from screaming.

Lena tossed her head. "I showed him. He knew he was dying. Then he wanted me to help. But I couldn't. I was a cold, calculating bitch, remember? He wanted his pills. I told him to get them himself."

Haley couldn't believe the words coming out of her mother's mouth. She'd killed two men—and no matter what he'd done, her father hadn't deserved to die that way—and now she was trying to kill them. All of a sudden, Haley realized how close to death she and Mack were.

She grabbed her cell phone and started to dial 9-1-1 when Lena suddenly screamed and launched herself at Haley. Before Haley knew it, her mother had snatched the phone from her hand and stomped it into pieces.

"You're not telling anyone else!" Lena screamed. "You're not telling! I won't let you!" She doubled up her fist and hit Haley on the side of the face, knocking her backward onto the floor.

Haley was struggling to her feet when she saw the lighter in Lena's hand.

"No! Mother, don't! For God's sake, don't!" she screamed, but Lena was already running.

Haley chased her through the living room, frantic to catch her before it was too late.

But Lena beat her to the door. When she turned, she was laughing and the lighter was lit. She dropped it onto the floor and then slammed the front door between them.

Haley gasped as the carpet runner exploded into flames. That was when she realized her mother had poured a trail of paint thinner all the way through the living room on her way into the kitchen. Now she only had seconds to get back to Mack and get them both outside before the house was engulfed.

Haley ran as fast as she'd ever run in her life. She could

hear the *whoosh* as the thinner continued to catch fire, but she couldn't think about what was behind her. She had to focus on Mack.

She grabbed him beneath his arms and tried to lift him out of the chair, but he was almost deadweight.

"Mack! Mack! You have to help me!" she cried, and then raised his head and slapped him in the face.

The jolt roused Mack enough that she got him to his feet.

"Run!" she screamed. "We have to run! Now! The house is on fire!"

Mack could hear Haley screaming, but his mind was so fuzzy that he couldn't understand why. He tried to move, but his legs felt like lead.

When he slumped against her again, Haley groaned. The fire was coming through the hall. When it got to the kitchen, it would be over.

She grabbed Mack's arm, slung it around her shoulder, then grabbed him tight against her and started running. She got them to the back door and got it open just as the fire entered the kitchen. She was dragging him across the back porch as the kitchen literally exploded. Windows shattered, sending glass flying into the air and flames licking up the sides of the house.

"Move, Mack! Move! We have to keep moving!" she screamed, and got them both out into the yard before he collapsed at her feet. She was on her knees, gasping for breath, when the first neighbor came running.

"Call the fire department!" Haley cried.

"Already did," the neighbor said.

"Then call the police and an ambulance. There's an arsonist on the run."

Haley didn't know the man, but he quickly obliged. She heard him making the calls as she kept dragging Mack farther away from the house. She got him all the way around the side of the house and across the front yard, then down to the end of the driveway. By the time she got him to the street, she was sobbing. She sat down on the curb and cradled Mack's head in her lap while the world burned up behind them.

Chief Bullard arrived just behind the ambulance. He ran up as Haley was talking to the paramedics.

"I'm not sure what was in the brownies she gave him, but it knocked him out. I had to drag him out of the house." Then she pointed to his arm and started to cry again. "I think I tore some of his stitches loose, but there wasn't time to—"

Bullard put a hand on Haley's shoulder. "Haley?"

She turned, saw the concern and confusion on his face and started to talk in what must have sounded like crazy ramblings.

"My mother…she doped the brownies Mack ate. He was unconscious when I got back to the house. She kept talking about not telling her secret and that no one could know. Then she set fire to the house."

"Lord have mercy!" Bullard said.

"That's not all," Haley said, and drew a deep, shuddering breath. "She knew Tom Brolin was allergic to bees. She threw a bunch of them into his vehicle and watched him die."

"What? Wait! Are you saying she—"

"And she and my father had a fight. When he started having a heart attack, she wouldn't get his medicine. She watched him die, begging her for help."

"Good Lord! Do you hear what you're saying? Why on earth would she do that?"

"Because of Stewart. Because Stewart wasn't Judd's son. He was Tom's…and she kept killing people to keep her secret and hide her shame."

Bullard was dumbstruck. "Where is she?"

"I don't know," Haley said. "She must have gotten in her car and driven away. I don't think she's in her right mind," she added.

"After all of this, neither do I," Bullard said, then changed the subject.

"Are you gonna be okay? Is there anyone I can call?"

Haley choked on a sob, then almost smiled. "I'm sure in your job that you've heard this before, but whatever you do... don't call my mother."

At that point, Bullard had heard enough. He pulled her into his arms and just held her. And when the ambulance drove off with Mack Brolin inside, he loaded Haley into his cruiser and took her to the hospital.

By the time they arrived, he'd already issued a BOLO for Lena Shore.

"Go be with Mack," he told Haley. "If we hear anything, I'll come find you."

"Thank you," she said. "For everything."

Then she jumped out of the car and started running. She got inside just as they were pumping Mack's stomach.

Haley was sitting at Mack's bedside, watching him sleep, when the door burst open and his sisters ran in. Haley stood abruptly, bracing herself for a fight that never came.

Jenna started crying as Carla launched herself into Haley's arms.

"They told us what you did...that you carried him out of the house all by yourself." Carla sobbed. "You saved his life again, Haley, and we're so thankful. So very, very thankful!"

Haley couldn't believe it. Obviously they hadn't heard the whole story.

"My mother is the one who set the fire," she said.

"We know. Chief Bullard told us. He told us everything. Poor Dad. Mom never knew. None of us knew."

Haley heard Mack beginning to stir. He'd been waking up off and on for the past hour, and although she'd told him what had happened, she wasn't sure if he would remember it. She turned and headed for the bed as he began to mumble her name.

"I'm here," Haley said. "Your sisters are here, too."

Mack frowned, then tried to sit up.

"Don't!" Jenna cried. "Lie back down, Mack. It's okay. Everything is okay. As long as you and Haley are alive, nothing else matters."

He frowned groggily. "That's quite an about-face."

Jenna was weeping loudly. "I'm sorry. Please. You have to forgive us. We're all one another has."

Carla chimed in. "We love you, Mack. And we'll be forever grateful to Haley. She's saved your life twice. If she'll forgive us, we want to be a family again."

Haley blinked back tears as she looked at Mack.

"Do you remember what happened?" she asked.

"Some of it."

"The house is gone. Mother burned it to the ground."

"It's insured," Mack said.

"But all your work…" she said.

"Brought you back to me," Mack finished for her, and sat up, then swung his legs over the side of the bed as Haley walked into his arms.

Mack sighed. He was still a little groggy, but that would wear off. Just knowing he had Haley was all the medicine he needed.

Then there was a knock on the door. They all turned to look as Chief Bullard walked in.

Haley could tell by the look on his face that it wasn't good.

"Did you find my mother?"

Bullard nodded.

"Where?"

"At the cemetery."

Haley shuddered, then swallowed past the lump in her throat. "She's dead, isn't she?"

He nodded. "Shot herself on your brother's grave."

"Oh, my God," Haley said. "Oh, my God. All this hate. All the lives lost…and all because of a secret she didn't want told."

"I'm so sorry, Haley," the chief said. "I'll…I'll leave you alone now. If there's anything else I need, I'll be in touch later," he said, as he walked out the door.

Suddenly Mack's arms were around her, holding her close. Mack's sisters surrounded the two of them, hugging and crying along with her.

"It's gonna be all right, Haley. It's gonna be all right," Mack said. "We're alive and healthy, and we have each other. Nothing else matters."

"And you both have us," Carla added.

Mack cupped Haley's face and tilted her head until their gazes were locked.

"Look at me," he said softly.

"I'm looking," Haley whispered.

"What do you see?"

She sighed as an odd sort of peace began to spill through her.

"I see my future. I see the man I'm going to grow old with. I've spent my life fighting for the right to love you. " Then she looked at Mack. "What do *you* see?"

"I see the woman who holds my heart and my life in her hands. Tell me you're still going to marry me."

"Yes."

"And live with me in the big house with the big bed."

Haley almost smiled. "Yes."

"Then it's all been worth it," he said, then turned to his sisters. "Somebody go find a doctor. We're ready to go home."

Haley buried her face against Mack's chest. She thought of her old apartment back in Dallas, and the trio of locks she'd needed to keep herself safe. She wouldn't be needing that kind of protection anymore.

She'd spent her entire life fighting for the right to love him, and she would do it all over again if she had to.

Some things in life were meant to be, and Mack Brolin was meant to be hers.

* * * * *

LETHAL LESSONS

BY
COLLEEN THOMPSON

This one's for my mother-in-law, Orpha Thompson.
Your warmth and generosity have meant
the world to me.

But the Woman that God gave him, every fibre of her frame
Proves her launched for one sole issue, armed and engined
for the same,
And to serve that single issue, lest the generations fail,
The female of the species must be deadlier than the male.

—Rudyard Kipling,
"The Female of the Species"

Chapter 1

In the crowded parking lot of Red Bluff Elementary, Mara Stillwell climbed out of the First Big Change in her life, a used, blue Mini Cooper she had bought on impulse after the big breakup. Stomach fluttering, she stared at the Second Big Change: an Arizona sunset so spectacular it made her want to dip a brush into its vibrant colors. At the horizon's western edge, the sun slid behind jagged rock formations that took her breath away each time she chanced to look up.

"Oh, Mara," she whispered to herself. "I've a feeling we're not in Jersey anymore."

Removed from her former drab surroundings, Mara felt less drab herself, with part of the credit going to the pretty turquoise-and-white summer dress and sandals she'd bought for the "meet the teacher" evening that preceded her first day at her new school. She doubted Jerry the Jackass would even know her, with her newly auburn hair brushed straight and shining past her shoulders, and her thick-framed glasses traded for a set of contacts that didn't hide her green eyes.

Here in her new home, no one would recognize her—or whisper about the fiancé who'd been hauled off by the police only a few weeks before she'd planned to marry him this past June. The fiancé—make that *ex*-fiancé—who'd made it impossible for her to live and work in her hometown.

Which was why Mara felt so stunned to look down from the stage where she sat with the other members of the faculty and see a familiar face among the waiting parents in the auditorium. A still-amazing face, all these years after she had last seen Adam Jakes, her older brother Trace's best friend throughout high school.

Unbelievably, her stomach did that same stupid flip-flop it had when she was twelve and the sixteen-year-old god of Sea Shores High School sailed into a room and claimed it, filling it with his running-back-tight body, his thick, dark hair and darker eyes. Eyes that seemed to read the fine print on her prepubescent soul.

A wave of heat crashed over her, reminding her how hard she had fallen and how many nights she'd cried in her bed, suffering the pangs of what her mother had dismissed as "puppy love."

Adam was even better looking now, the promise of his youthful features fully realized, his chest and shoulders unmistakably defined beneath the polo shirt he wore with khaki slacks and what looked, even from this distance, like an expensive watch and shoes. Though his family had had little money, she should have known he would wind up not only handsome but successful—and happily married, she guessed, judging from the adorable child beside him, a little girl of about seven, with waist-length, sun-streaked hair held back by a headband that matched her pink sundress.

"You're blushing, Mara," whispered Pippa Kelly, the school's only other second-grade teacher. A few years older than Mara's thirty, she'd been so friendly and helpful that Mara couldn't resent her wholesome blond prettiness or how happy she, her husband and their six-year-old twins had seemed when they'd invited Mara to a backyard barbecue last week to welcome her to town. "Don't worry. The parents here are going to love you."

Jillian Rhodes, the principal who had hired Mara, stepped up to the podium, her expectant smile soon quieting all conversation. Polished and professional in her crisp summer suit and slingbacks, Mrs. Rhodes peered over stylish reading glasses and welcomed the parents and students to an exciting new school term.

"And this year I'm delighted to introduce a gifted educator we've been lucky enough to lure all the way from Sea Shores, New Jersey, where she was named her district's teacher of the year. Please help me extend a warm, Red Bluff welcome to Miss Mara Stillwell, our newest addition to the second grade."

Mara felt her blush deepen as Mrs. Rhodes gestured for her to stand up to a polite round of applause. Applause and what looked like astonishment in the handsome gaze now latched on to hers.

Please don't let Trace have called or written and told him about what happened, she prayed. *Please don't let me start my new life in Red Bluff as an object of pity and suspicion.*

No way, Adam Jakes thought as he studied the blushing knockout rising from the line of chairs. There was no way that was his old friend Trace's pesky little sister, she of the skinned knees, stick figure and hideous glasses. But despite the dazzling green eyes and a set of curves her modest dress couldn't disguise, the mention of his hometown short-circuited his knee-jerk denial.

This Mara Stillwell—the same Miss Stillwell who'd been listed as his daughter's teacher—could only be the girl who'd annoyed the devil out of him with her moony stares and obvious adoration. As gorgeous as she'd turned out, she would probably get a real laugh from that now—or maybe a shiver, once she heard the ugly rumors swirling around his wife's death, as was sure to happen in no time flat.

Dread coiled in his gut, and he wished uselessly that Mara didn't have to hear the speculation. Wished he could somehow go back in time to those days when he'd been nothing but poor—and a little girl's first crush.

Soon Jillian Rhodes' rah-rah introduction to the faculty ended and the teachers were free to leave the stage and mingle with the parents and students.

Bending to look at his daughter, Rebecca, he dredged up a smile he wasn't feeling. "Ready to say hello, sweetie?"

She shrugged indifferently, her face too world-weary for one so young. Since her mother's death a year ago, the child's natural bubbliness had spiraled into a troubling near-silence that robbed him of sleep and filled his waking thoughts. Shouldn't Rebecca be getting better instead of sliding deeper into darkness? If he were any sort of father, wouldn't he have pulled his head out of his work, his own refuge from grief, and found some way to reach her by now?

"Hey, I've got an idea." Adam kept his voice deliberately upbeat. "Let's get your teacher some punch from the refreshment table. She'll probably be thirsty by the time she finishes talking with all the other kids and parents."

He offered the plan as a way to avoid the initial press, along with the potential stares that would be so hard for both him and his daughter. He especially wanted to steer clear of PTO president Barbara Fairmont, who, hot on the heels of her latest divorce, had called and left several messages asking him to join her on some committee.

But Adam had heard the subtext, the implication that she would be willing to look past his recent "misfortune" for a chance to hook up with *his* fortune—or at the very least enjoy a few nights in his bed. *Not a chance in hell,* he thought, picturing his head hung as a trophy on her wall of vanquished exes. Or maybe it wasn't the *heads* she was collecting....

Wincing at the thought, he turned away to fill cups with punch and wait with his daughter until Mara Stillwell finished her last conversation.

When she spotted him, her full lips curved into a smile that didn't quite touch her eyes. "Adam Jakes," she said. "I never imagined I'd find a fellow Seahorse out here."

Grinning at the memory of their high school's "Mighty Seahorse" mascot, he dryly quoted the old war cry, "Seahorse Stampede!" and offered one of the two paper cups in his hands.

Accepting with thanks, Mara laughed at his foolishness, then crouched to bring herself close to Rebecca's level. As she offered her free hand in greeting, Mara said, "And who is this bright-looking young lady?"

Ignoring her teacher's hand, Rebecca stared down at her own sandals, and Adam felt a familiar pang in his chest. *Please don't think my kid's rude. Or socially retarded.*

"Rebecca's feeling a little shy right now," he said in one of the great understatements of the decade.

"That's okay, Rebecca." Mara let her hand drop. "I was shy, too, when I was your age. I'm sure your daddy will be only too happy to give you some *really* embarrassing examples."

Adam thought he saw a tiny smile, though Rebecca still refused eye contact. Grateful for Mara's kindness, he said, "You're pretty far inland for a Seahorse. What brings you here to Red Bluff?"

Something that might have been pain flashed over her face, but it was quickly plastered over.

"Well, I'd just turned thirty," she said lightly, "and I suddenly felt as if my potential for adventure was about to reach its expiration date. So I started searching for teaching positions anywhere that sounded exotic. Once I saw the pictures of the hiking and ballooning and all that gorgeous red rock, I emailed my application before I could chicken out and change my mind."

Adam studied her for a moment, struck by the story's charm and polish. *Rehearsed,* some instinct warned him, but he told himself it was probably only that she'd repeated it a lot lately. "How'd your family take that?"

Mara smiled again. "Trace is probably still asking himself what got into me, but since he's serving in Afghanistan, what's he really going to say?"

"Still an army man, then?"

"A captain now. Dad would've been so proud if he had lived to see it."

Out of the corner of his eye, Adam saw Barbara Fairmont gliding their way on vamp-red, spike-heeled sandals, her skin tanned and hair freshly lightened to her famous on-the-prowl blond. He spotted several of the dads checking her out and caught a few irritated glances from the women, although one eagerly buzzed "I'd love to help you decorate for next month's tea" to the queen bee.

Taking advantage of the distraction, Adam told Mara, "It's been great catching up, but I'm afraid Rebecca and I need to hurry home now. Early morning tomorrow, what with the first day of school."

"I enjoyed meeting you, Rebecca. And it was a nice surprise seeing you again, Adam." Mara shook his hand, sending an unexpected jolt of recognition arcing through his body.

Focused on his daughter, Adam was able to escape without meeting Barbara Fairmont's gaze directly. But not without recognizing the flash of poison behind her bright blue eyes.

As the last parents and children straggled out, Mara headed toward the door in the company of several other teachers. She was eager to get home to the little guesthouse, which the locals called a casita, that she was renting. But she smiled as the PTO president, an attractive blonde in red heels, clicked toward her. Pippa had already warned Mara that Barbara Fairmont would watch her every move these first months, and that she and Principal Rhodes were close friends.

Neither piece of news worried Mara. She knew everyone would be carefully scrutinizing her this first semester, but she knew, too, that she would soon win over both her students and their parents. Because Mara had realized early on that she had a gift for teaching, a talent for motivating kids to achieve their potential and for reaching children who would otherwise slip through the cracks.

She would have no trouble whatsoever—as long as Adam Jakes didn't take it upon himself to call his old friend Trace overseas.

"I'm looking forward to meeting Cody in the morning," Mara told Barbara now, a bit surprised the woman hadn't brought her son this evening. "I hope he's all set for a great new school year."

Ignoring the comment, Mrs. Fairmont asked her, "You know Adam Jakes?"

There was an edge in the question, a challenge Mara didn't understand. But she saw no reason to deny it. "Yes, can you believe it? He's an old friend of my brother's. I lost track of him years ago. I had no idea he'd moved out here."

But Mara was beginning to wonder if she *had* heard something about it a few years earlier, back home. If that might be the reason the name "Red Bluff" had jumped out at her when she'd been scouring the internet for job leads. Perhaps their surprise meeting was less than the pure coincidence she'd first thought.

Jillian Rhodes came up to them then, her glasses perched atop her short, frosted brown hair.

Barbara Fairmont's gaze snapped to meet Jillian's. "Our Miss Stillwell grew up with Adam Jakes. But she doesn't know about…" Sleek eyebrows a shade darker than her blond locks lifted suggestively before she finished with "…his wife."

Mara tilted her head, looking from one woman to the other. She had assumed Adam was married, of course, but now it sounded as if there was more to the story.

"Mrs. Jakes died in an accident last year," the principal said carefully. Too carefully. "A terrible tragedy. She…fell. Hiking around the cliffs near their home."

"After midnight," commented Barbara Fairmont so quietly Mara barely heard it.

"How horrible," said Mara. "That poor little girl, poor family. Are there any other children?"

Jillian Rhodes looked troubled as she answered, "Just Rebecca."

"No wonder she's so quiet." Mara had been fourteen when a car wreck claimed her mother, but she well remembered how lost she had felt. How very alone in her grief, though her father and brother were both devastated, too. "Thanks for letting me know. I'll do everything I can to help her."

Mrs. Rhodes nodded her approval. "Please go on ahead. I need to make sure we're all locked up."

Outside, the stars blazed overhead, so many more than had ever been visible from Mara's hometown. It smelled different here, too, the marshy-brine odor of dead sea grass replaced by the lightly floral clarity of the high desert. To Mara, the air felt charged with promise.

Walking beside her, Mrs. Fairmont whispered, "You need to be careful. All that looking up, you're sure to miss the scorpions."

"Oh." Mara glanced down past her sandals, but the security lights along the walkway showed nothing to alarm her. "They're nocturnal, then?"

"Oh, yes, just like our tarantulas. But never hikers. No one walks the cliffs after midnight. Especially not the cheating wives of rich real-estate developers."

Mara stopped short. She hated gossip, especially the kind of sly insinuation that had all but run her out of town. *I can't imagine her not knowing what he was up to. What if she—oh, my, I hate to even think this, but…*

"So you're saying you think something…" Mara couldn't keep the edge from her voice. "You're suggesting Mrs. Jakes committed suicide?"

Barbara Fairmont shook her head. "Oh, no. No one seriously believes Christine Jakes took her own life."

Shock rippled through Mara's body, wave after wave. Because the alternative was impossible to fathom, especially in this gorgeous little town, with its pastel adobe houses and its spectacular red rock vistas. "Then you're suggesting someone *pushed* her? You mean— Has there been an investigation?"

Poor Adam.

Mrs. Fairmont gave a little laugh. "You don't understand. People around here are tired of being 'Arizona's best-kept secret.' The resort Adam Jakes is building is going to put this place on the map, just the way he did for that little California town where he made himself a big name. We're talking millions of tourist dollars pumped into Red Bluff, and no one wants to jeopardize—"

"I'm not sure I want to hear this." Mara's face burned, and a buzzing started in her ears.

"He's an important man in this town. Almost untoucha—"

"I was wrong. I *am* sure," Mara interrupted. "I prefer starting every school year fresh and forming my own opinions of each student."

"How commendable," Mrs. Fairmont said flatly before pointing out an inch-long scorpion that had wandered onto the path between them, its tail and stinger arched above its back. "But when you're in unfamiliar territory, it does pay to be cautious. At least until you figure out the lay of the land."

With the slightest smile, she lifted one red sandal and crushed out the tiny creature like a burning cigarette.

Chapter 2

With the knock at the door, the fuzzy gray-and-white kitten somersaulted off the sofa with a squeak of surprise. Laughing at his theatrics, Mara coughed into her tissue—a noisy remnant of the upper respiratory infection that had kept her home for the past two days.

She was tempted to play dead, but another knock convinced her she'd been heard, or else the Beethoven playing on her iPod speakers had given her away. Reluctantly, she put down the papers she'd been grading and peered through her front door's peephole.

Adam Jakes stood on the other side, looking so perfect in his crisp, rolled-sleeve shirt and khakis that embarrassment ignited her face. She couldn't believe he'd stopped by without warning, especially on a day when her nose was red, her hair a disaster and she was wearing the same ratty pink bathrobe she'd had on all day, though it was past six on a Friday afternoon.

Well, she reminded herself, she'd been telling herself for

three months that she should discourage his attentions. If this didn't frighten him off, she wasn't sure what would.

Opening the door, she smiled to see Rebecca standing beneath the level of the peephole with her skinny arm extended, offering a hand-painted get-well card.

"I made this for you." The child's thin voice trembled. "To help you get better so you can come and teach me."

"Why, thank you, Rebecca. What a nice surprise." Mara felt a flush of warmth unrelated to her cold. For Rebecca to dare to come here, to initiate a conversation, was an incredible achievement.

Adam stood a few steps behind her, carrying a paper grocery sack.

Pleasure lit his dark eyes, along with unmistakable male interest. An interest Pippa had warned Mara she would do well to ignore, considering the community's double standards regarding the behavior of its teachers.

Good advice, thought Mara, especially in light of the static she'd been getting from the principal. Avoiding Adam's stare, she looked at the card she'd just accepted. "This is beautiful."

Using the technique Mara had taught her in one of their private, after-school art sessions, Rebecca had created a watercolor sunset imbued with sparkling glitter. She'd written the words *get well soon* above a jagged black ridge meant to represent the silhouetted local rocks.

Mara recognized the outline of a bluff Rebecca drew into every picture. A bluff that Adam had confirmed resembled the two-hundred-foot drop-off where the girl's mother had died.

Mara shivered at the thought of Rebecca's recent drawings, which had included a tiny figure tumbling off the edge. More disturbing still, Mara had watched the girl at work, her pale eyes growing glassy and unfocused as she worked. If asked about her art, she would turn tearful, ripping up the picture and crying "You hate it!"

Adam gently told his daughter, "We need to leave the card and let her rest now."

"Thank you, both of you," said Mara. "I'm feeling much better already. I'm over the contagious part and expect to be back at school on Monday morning."

"We really shouldn't have disturbed you, but when Rebecca asked..." His dark brows rose, acknowledging his one weakness—he could deny his child nothing. And hinting, too, that he had been aware that Mara's kindness to his daughter had gone beyond professional concern.

Just as Mara was unnaturally aware of everything about him, from the speculation in his brown eyes whenever they spoke to the way his muscles gathered, strong and firm, beneath the surface of his skin when he moved. As he moved now, to pass the bag in her direction.

"Careful," he said. "It's hot."

"Excuse me?"

"Chicken soup. I had Mrs. Somers make her magic recipe. It'll have you on your feet in no time."

Mara had met his housekeeper, a regal, graying woman who invariably wore pearls and nodded stiffly when she stopped by the classroom to pick up Rebecca on those days when Adam couldn't make it.

"That's very kind, but—" Mara started as the kitten, only ten weeks old and ornery, slipped through the open door and scampered into the rock garden that separated the casita from the main house.

"You have a kitty." Rebecca lit up, staring after him.

"His name's Jasper," Mara said. "Do you think you could keep him company for a few minutes? He'd love to play with you."

Rebecca looked to her father, who nodded and said, "Just stay where I can see you."

Once Rebecca was out of earshot, Mara glanced down at the bag he offered. "You didn't have to do this."

"Maybe I *wanted* to," Adam insisted, his unrelenting focus setting off a pleasant round of shivers. "To wish you a quick recovery and as a thank-you for all you're doing for Rebecca."

Mara lifted her palms. "I've told you, seeing your daughter blossom is thanks enough," she said, but her stomach did that nervous flip-flop that told her she was lying to herself. That they'd both been lying, pretending it was no more than their shared concern for the subject of Rebecca's artwork that had him lingering longer and longer after school to discuss her progress.

"It's just soup, Mara," he said, his smile teasing.

Though she knew better, she accepted the bag anyway. As she set it on the straight-backed wooden chair beside the door, she thought of other offerings dropped by her classroom, from a wind-sculpted piece of desert wood to a beautifully striated rock to local piñon candies. Little things, she'd told herself. Things that didn't matter. Still, she felt their tendrils winding tight around her heart.

"I know you mean well," she told him, "but this is going to have to stop. People have already noticed the visits to my classroom. If someone sees you coming here, too…"

"How would that be any of their business? We're two unattached adults, two people both concerned about my daughter. If we want to be friends—"

"I'm Rebecca's teacher," she cut in. "There's a line there, and I want to be sure I stay on the right side of it. Especially with the principal watching me like a hawk."

"Mrs. Rhodes? Why would she? I'd think she'd be delighted to have hired such an excellent new teacher."

Mara shook her head and frowned. "She's a back-to-basics educator—and no fan of innovation. Wants me to stick with drills and rote memorization, and forget about what she calls 'all that touchy-feely nonsense.'"

Mara still couldn't believe that the same techniques that had made her teacher of the year back in New Jersey had gotten her into hot water here.

"But that's ridiculous," Adam said. "Anyone can see those kids are happy and they're learning. Rebecca's responding in a way she's never—"

"I know, but I can't get Mrs. Rhodes to read the research links I sent her, and she couldn't care less that my students wouldn't think of missing school." With an ironic smile, she tapped her red nose. "Even when they're germy."

"What if I went in and spoke to her? I could talk to some of the other parents, get them to back you up."

"Don't, Adam, please. You'll only make things worse."

They both turned at the sound of Rebecca's laughter, which was aimed at the kitten, who was leaping wildly at a stick the girl was dragging through the white stones near the back wall.

"Careful around those cacti," Mara warned.

"She's lived here since she was two. She knows," Adam assured her. "But what do you mean, I'll only make things worse?"

Mara didn't answer. Didn't want to say.

"What is it? Has Mrs. Rhodes already warned you off me?" Raw anger flashed over his face, a bolt of pain slashing through a field of darkness. "Warned you people think that I'm some kind of mur—that my wife—"

"Of course she didn't say that." *That would be Barbara Fairmont.* But the PTO president was one problem Mara didn't want to discuss. "I only meant that Mrs. Rhodes wouldn't take it kindly if you called her judgment into question. Besides, I intend to prove to her my methods work. Pippa Kelly's interested, too, so we decided to conduct a little experiment.

We're going to check the two classes' progress side by side."

"But that would mean you're still using your—"

Mara put a finger to her smiling lips and gave him a meaningful look. "Things will work themselves out. But until they do, please, no more presents. And let's try to keep our conversations focused on Rebecca."

Behind her, the lamp flickered out as the *Moonlight* Sonata died midnote.

Adam looked over his shoulder. "Lights are still on in the main house."

Mara shook her head, annoyed with the all-too-frequent inconvenience. "It's the wiring in this old place. It's very temperamental."

Concern furrowed his forehead. "It's also very dangerous. And look, right here. These are pry marks near your door lock. And they're fresh, judging from the way these paint chips are still hanging."

Studying them, Mara shivered.

Had someone tried to break in? If so, it must have happened while she'd been at the doctor's office. Otherwise, she surely would have heard it. A fresh chill skated up the back of her neck. Last night she'd fallen asleep listening to music with her headphones. On the sofa, less than ten feet from the door.

She hugged herself tightly. "That's a little creepy. Do you think—should I call the police?"

"No police here. It would be the sheriff." He frowned before adding, "But let me look around first, see if there's anything else."

He took a few minutes to walk the guesthouse's perimeter before returning. "I don't see any other signs. Whoever damaged the door must've either slipped through the gate and past the main house, or he scaled the back wall."

She nodded, looking at the spiny, desert-hardy plantings that lined the concrete-block wall surrounding her landlord's backyard. "Front entrance, I'd imagine. Guess I should report this."

"Absolutely, you should. There might not be anything they can do, but they should know there's been an attempted break-in. Meanwhile, I'll get hold of your landlord, see that he locks that gate tonight. He'll need a deadbolt and a chain installed, too. Plus, the circuits are fried back there—whole box'll have to be replaced before you get your power back."

Heat rushed to her cheeks at the mention of her landlord. "Maybe I should hire a handyman, get things replaced myself. If my landlord fixes this place up, he'll raise the rent sky high."

The crumbling, one-bedroom adobe was the best she could afford, and she'd been lucky to find it. Besides, few places would allow her to keep her kitten.

"No, he won't. I know Enrique. Don't worry, I'll see to it," Adam told her in a voice that brooked no argument. "I'll just send over a small crew and an electrician. They'll take care of it in half a day or so on Monday, but first thing tomorrow morning, I'll have a generator and some power cords brought out so you can run your lights and the refrigerator."

Mara reminded herself she wasn't on his payroll. Nor was she a lovesick twelve-year-old.

"That's very kind, very generous," she said firmly. "But it wouldn't be appropriate. I'll replace the locks myself and—"

"Forget about it, Mara." Adam smiled. "I'll take care of everything."

As he collected his daughter and walked away, Mara could almost hear Barbara Fairmont hissing *The same way you took care of your wife?*

His dead wife, Christine, the mother that Rebecca kept drawing in midair as she fell.

Ridiculous, thought Mara as she closed and locked the door. She might be annoyed at Adam for putting her in an uncomfortable position, but she didn't for a moment buy that he'd disposed of his wife on the dark bluffs near his mansion. Sure, he might be a little intense at times, a little too used to having people jump to satisfy his orders, but the news articles she'd looked up gave no hint that his wife's death had been anything more than a tragic accident. More important, any idiot could see he would never hurt his child by killing her mother. He would never murder anyone—not even a wife rumored to have been unfaithful.

Besides, Barbara Fairmont was nothing but a vicious gossip, a woman who somehow attracted a clique of followers and used them to keep all lesser beings in line.

Not surprisingly, her overweight, unhappy son was every bit as much of a bully. Mara had been quick to hold Cody accountable and was working hard to win him over, but his mother's resistance was seriously undercutting the boy's progress. No doubt Barbara was complaining to her good friend Jillian Rhodes, too, fueling the principal's dislike for Mara.

After dishing out a fragrant bowl of soup, Mara settled in to eat by candlelight. As she enjoyed the delicious warmth, she reminded herself firmly that she'd come here to escape gossip, not become the center of it at yet another school.

So I'll call Adam tomorrow, when we can talk like two adults, not parent and teacher. I'll tell him no work crews, no presents and that I'm perfectly capable of handling a few small problems.

That decided, she finished dinner and looked up the nonemergency number for the sheriff's department, where she ended up routed to someone's voice mail. "Huh," she told Jasper after stammering through a brief message. "They really do roll up the sidewalks in this burg after sundown."

Maybe Red Bluff really was as safe as she'd been told when she had moved here. Still, before she turned in, she propped a chair beneath the sole door and slept fitfully, her cell phone by her side in the darkened house.

"I'm not sure I'm hearing you right," Mara's landlord, Enrique Trejo, told Adam on the phone. An entrepreneur in his own right—his family operated the popular Roadrunner Café—he seemed confused by Adam's offer. "What's in this for you? Unless... Don't tell me you've got a little something going with *la maestra bonita?*"

It didn't surprise Adam that he wasn't the only man in town who'd noticed the pretty new schoolteacher. What really astonished him was his own interest, a capacity he would have sworn had been lost—burned away forever—after Christine's death.

Guilt razored his conscience. It had been only fifteen months, fifteen months since he'd jolted awake to an empty bed.

"Mara's an old friend, that's all." Adam slid off the edge of the desk where he'd been leaning and paced the confines of his spacious, mesquite-and-iron home office. Though the huge window overlooked the finest view in town, he paid no heed to the stars now emerging by the thousands, nor to the town's lights shining from below. "Or, I should say, her big brother was a good friend back in high school. He's serving overseas now, and he's her only family, so I thought maybe I should—"

"Keep an eye on her, amigo?"

"Exactly," Adam agreed, though he wasn't sure he liked the way Enrique had said it. "Which is why I'm sending over a work crew and an electrician Monday morning."

"And for this humanitarian effort, all I have to do is promise not to raise her rent this school year?"

"Let's make it the next *two* years," Adam pressed.

"For you, I say yes, because my wife likes the little *maestra* living in our backyard."

"Great. My guys'll be over with that generator first thing tomorrow. Meanwhile—"

"I'll lock up like you asked and watch out for her," Enrique promised, but in his voice Adam heard his conviction that no man would go to so much trouble for a woman whose bed he'd never shared or didn't plan to.

Adam wasn't quite sure he bought it, either, but for the moment, he trained his total focus on keeping Mara safe.

Chapter 3

When Mara pulled in to the parking lot on Saturday afternoon, she frowned at the expensive cars clustered near the school's entrance. Must be a PTO committee meeting for next Saturday's carnival, she imagined, as she eyed Barbara Fairmont's black BMW. They were probably holed up in the library, where they normally met.

Though Mara was feeling much better, thanks to either the antibiotics or Mrs. Somers' magic soup, she pulled around back in the hope of avoiding detection. She'd come to finish her lesson plans and didn't want to get sidetracked.

She especially didn't want to walk into a conversation about *her,* since the queen bee was officiating. Mara shuddered, imagining how much worse things would be if word ever got out about her fiancé's arrest.

Ex-fiancé, she thought, surprised to find the memory was no longer quite as painful. Maybe after eight months it had finally sunk in how lucky she'd been to dodge the bullet of that marriage. Or maybe her new home had come to be more to her than an escape route, despite its challenges.

Including Adam Jakes, whose persuasion had had her landlord insisting on the offered repairs. She'd tried to explain to Enrique why she couldn't accept, but he'd said, "You don't understand. He's doing me the favor. Carlota's been after me to fix up the casita for years, but we're always so busy with the café. So please, *señorita,* for the sake of your safety and my marriage…"

Reluctantly, Mara had agreed, but the arrangement made her nervous. How would it look if the PTO brigade or Mrs. Rhodes heard Adam was doing all this for her?

Mara used her key to unlock the back breezeway gate and walked into the ring of numbered doors, which were arranged in a circle around a grassy central courtyard. It still seemed odd to her to teach in a school where all the classrooms opened straight to the outdoors, though precipitation was so rare here, the weather hardly ever made the unusual layout a problem.

She gathered up her papers and was finishing her plans when someone tapped at her door. "There is no escape," she mumbled, figuring one of the moms had seen her car.

Instead, it was a dad. When she opened the door, Adam Jakes was standing there looking handsome as sin in a fatigue-style shirt and jeans that fit him in a way schoolteachers weren't supposed to notice.

He grinned down at her, looking all too aware of the childish crush he'd resurrected. "Hey there, feeling any better? You're looking good."

"Much better, thank you. Though I'm sure anything's an improvement over the red nose and pink bathrobe."

"My fault for showing up unannounced. And I'm kind of partial to a woman in terrycloth."

She frowned to cover the blasted blush that followed. "What brings you here on a Saturday?"

He hooked a thumb in the direction of the library. "Caught

in the flypaper. Babzilla conned me into thinking there'd be a slew of dads up here to work on carnival stuff. Instead, there's only me."

Mara nearly choked on laughter. "You call Barbara Fairmont Babzilla?"

A wicked grin lit his dark eyes. "Not to her face, believe me. So can I come in before I'm spotted? I told them I had to duck out for a call."

Stepping back, she sketched a curtsy. "I grant thee sanctuary. I needed to talk to you anyway."

"Sure, Mara." No "Miss Stillwater" here, with the door closing behind him. Closing the two of them in alone.

Palms damp as a nervous schoolgirl's, Mara was all too aware this was the first time in fifteen years—or possibly ever—that had happened. *Forget it,* she told herself. *Just remember what you have to tell him.* But it was tough to focus, with her hormones running around high-fiving each another like a bunch of cheerleaders.

She gave the squad a mental shake and willed herself to grow up. "I want to tell you how very much I appreciate what you've done, Adam. It's incredibly nice of you."

He slanted an amused look her way. "Do I hear a *but* in there?"

"I've enjoyed talking to you. I really have, but this attention's making me uncomfortable. *You* are, blurring the line between what I'm doing professionally for Rebecca and—"

"Wonders." Solemnity drove the playfulness from his voice. "You're doing *wonders* for her. It's unbelievable, the difference. I know she still has a long way to go, but some days, Mara, I think you've saved my daughter's life."

A stillness fell between them, a hush she measured in the ticking of the wall clock, the beating of her heart.

Do something, she told herself, *before this goes any further.*

"Children really are resilient" she heard herself saying.

"They're programmed for survival. A lot of Rebecca's recovery is only natural, a result of your love and patience and time."

He moved closer, so close she could smell the clean scent of his aftershave and feel the heat of him, a palpable presence against her sensitized skin. "You don't understand," he said. "Until late August, I could hardly get her to make eye contact, much less talk to anyone. I tried a counselor, a child psychologist—even a psychiatrist in Flagstaff who recommended medication. But when you started those art lessons…"

"It's gratitude you're feeling," Mara said, willing herself to take a step back but somehow going nowhere.

"Not just gratitude. Haven't you noticed how easy it is to talk and smile when we're together? You don't know the last time I laughed the way I did last week when you told me how that little boy complained Cody Fairmont had kicked him in his ovaries."

She grinned before reminding herself that Cody's bullying—and poor Jason's bruised testicles—were no laughing matter.

"I'm your child's teacher." She fought to still the quaver in her voice. "Not the little girl who used to follow you around and stare at you through Coke-bottle glasses."

"You think I see a little girl here?" He reached toward her face, his callused fingers skimming her cheek as he moved even closer. *Close enough to kiss,* she thought, her heartbeat picking up speed.

As he searched her eyes, she felt him looking for the slightest indication that she wanted what he wanted, what they had both wanted almost from the first moment they had reconnected.

But it was Adam who first pulled his hand from hers and turned away. "I'm sorry. It's still—this is crazy. It's way too soon for me to feel…what I *think* I'm feeling. It can't be real, not already."

"You mean after Christine."

He flinched to hear her name, so Mara laid her hand on his shoulder. "I'm sorry. It's only—I've been thinking the same thing. I was engaged, Adam. We were supposed to be married in June."

"I know," he told her.

"What? Did Trace…?"

Adam shook his head. "I still have some family back in Sea Shores. When I mentioned I'd run into you, my aunt told me."

In his expression, Mara saw that the woman must have mentioned the gossip in their hometown. Sickened and ashamed, she dropped her gaze. "How long have you known?"

He shrugged. "A couple months or so."

"But you didn't mention it to anyone?"

"Why would I? It wasn't your fault your fiancé turned out to be a thief."

"The worst kind." Seeing that Adam didn't know all of it, she explained, "He abused the trust his parents spent decades building in their furniture business. Stole their customers' identities from their credit applications. And snorted everything he stole up his nose."

Shaking her head, she added bitterly, "I didn't even have a clue he *used* drugs."

"He abused *your* trust, too," Adam emphasized. "And as far as I'm concerned, what happened is no one's business but yours. Heaven knows, I've found out this past year how much rumors hurt. And I don't for a minute believe you had anything to do with your ex's criminal behavior."

She looked up, capturing his gaze and captured by it at the same time, so she could barely find breath enough to speak. "I want you to know I feel exactly the same way. About you, I mean."

He turned away, his body tensing, but Mara had already

glimpsed the pain flashing through his eyes, a pain he usually covered, like a stone bruise to the soul.

She ran her palm along his forearm. "I'm so sorry. I just wanted you to know—"

Whether it was her touch or what she was saying, Adam turned abruptly and pulled her into his strong arms, claiming her mouth with a kiss that roared straight through her. There was nothing tentative or tame about it, nothing but the sear of heat and the taste of a lifetime's pent-up longing.

Forgetting where she was, *who* she was, Mara tilted back her head and gave in to the impulse, her lips parting to his questing tongue, a moan starting low in her throat. His hands inflamed her further, moving from her back to slide along the flare of her hips, then cup her buttocks and pull her even closer.

She ached inside, feeling the pressure of his hardness against her stomach…feeling herself, feeling both of them, swiftly losing control. And loving every second as he backed her against the desk, his hands fumbling to unbutton her top, then unhook her bra as he kissed his way down toward her aching nipples…

The door to her classroom swung open. "Adam Jakes, I thought I saw you heading this—"

The woman's gasp, the choked sound of her outrage, had Mara pulling away from Adam, turning to hide her bare breasts.

Too late. The damage had been done, as she heard Barbara Fairmont's furious, "You can absolutely *bet,* Miss Stillwell, that Jillian Rhodes will be hearing about your extracurricular activities."

Chapter 4

"Wait, Barbara," Adam called after the blonde as the woman's heels pounded a receding rhythm on the sidewalk. "You need to listen."

She wheeled to face him, her flaming face in stark contrast to today's poison-green ensemble. "If you're trying to explain, don't bother. Your actions have already done it for you. I've wondered for weeks about all your after-school visits to that classroom, especially since you've been *far too busy* to return my calls."

"I *am* busy. Trying to get the first phase of my project running and attempting to help my daughter move past what happened to her mother."

"Of course you are. And I take it our Miss Stillwell has been helping you. Offering her sympathy, as well as a soft—".

"There's no need to go there. Mara and I are both unattached adults. Two people who have known each other for a long time."

"Long enough to imagine she might have heard about your

money—and your recent widowhood. For all we know, she orchestrated this little reunion so she could—"

"She's done nothing of the sort," Adam insisted through clenched teeth. "She's a wonderful teacher and a fine woman."

Barbara rolled her eyes. "She's an absolute disaster. Trying to turn my Cody into a little priss."

Adam thought the kid, who'd spent most of first grade terrorizing Rebecca and others, could use a little milquetoast in his diet. Along with consistent discipline and possibly horse tranquilizers. But he held back, knowing Barbara could make life miserable for Mara. "Red Bluff's lucky to have her," he managed.

Something ugly settled into Barbara's gaze. "The way *you* were about to have her back in that classroom?"

"There's no need to be crude." Anger rumbled through his words, but he felt a stab of shame, too. What kind of man was he to have put a woman like Mara in such a situation? Their kiss had been explosive, burning every vestige of control from his mind, but she certainly deserved better than a hurried roll atop a hard metal desk. A hell of a lot better.

"I'm so sorry, Adam," Barbara told him, and to his shock, he saw tears in her eyes, vulnerability making her Botoxed beauty almost human. "Believe me, the last thing I want to do is quarrel. Especially with you… You have to know, as one of Christine's closest friends, I feel compelled to make certain you're—"

"One of Christine's *closest friends?*" That was news to him. He remembered his wife complaining about Barbara snubbing her offer to help out at some function.

Barbara shrugged and leaned forward, displaying those assets emphasized by her tight sweater. "Well, perhaps I overstated our relationship a little. But there's no exaggerating my compassion for your loss. I know what it's like to be alone, Adam. I know what it's like, and I despise it."

Through what he now realized were crocodile tears, she smiled at him, the predatory gleam in her eyes assuring him she wasn't about to let some brand-new teacher beat her to her intended target.

He warned her with a stern look. "I appreciate your... concern, but it's not necessary. And you should be aware that I consider Mara Stillwell a close friend."

Barbara opened her mouth, no doubt to say something cutting, but he didn't give her a chance.

"You go after her..." he said, "and you go after me. And I promise you, I'll take it *very* personally."

You ever come across a snarling dog, never turn your back and run, Mara's big brother had taught her, *'cause that's the quickest way to end up bleeding.*

With her face habanero hot, she wanted to flee anyway, or crawl into a hole somewhere to die. But her embarrassment was only temporary. If she turned tail rather than facing Barbara Fairmont, she might as well pack her bags and leave town now. And Mara was finished running. This time, if she went down, she swore she would do it fighting as bravely as her brother served their country.

She fixed her clothing, gathered her things, and left the classroom, just in time to hear Adam finish defending her to Barbara Fairmont. In the fierceness of his gaze and the harshness of his tone, Mara saw a strong protector, but his dark eyes softened the moment they found hers.

"Are you all right?" he asked.

"I'm fine." She sounded more confident than she felt. "And I'd like to apologize, Mrs. Fairmont. Certainly, what you witnessed was meant to be a private moment."

"In a *public* building," Barbara answered crisply before darting a nervous glance at Adam.

"Yes, and that was inappropriate. I'm sorry you were upset."

"It's unprofessional, Miss Stillwell. And it speaks volumes about your judgment. But…" Another glance at Adam, who was frowning, and she lifted her chin with a look of sheer defiance. "I'm willing to give you one more chance. Just keep in mind that I'll be watching. *Very* carefully."

"I understand." Mara forced herself to meet Barbara's gaze. "But I can assure you, I never make the same mistake twice."

"Then we'll just have to stay alert for new ones, won't we?" With that, the blonde spun on her heel and clicked her way back toward the front of the building.

Adam started after her, but Mara caught his arm. "That's enough, please. Don't make things any worse. I appreciate the way you stuck up for me, but it's really important that I deal with her myself."

He gave her an appraising look, new respect dawning in his eyes. Once Barbara disappeared into the library he said, "I'm very sorry, Mara. I never meant—I certainly didn't plan for anything like this to happen."

"It wasn't on my day's to-do list, either." She managed a smile. "But it's done now, and it definitely was *not* a good idea. That woman has the principal's ear, and you know Mrs. Rhodes is already on the fence about me."

"I still can't understand that."

"It doesn't matter right now. I just need to tell you—" Mara dragged in a steadying breath and gestured toward her classroom "—this *can't* happen again, Adam. It won't. Because even if I weren't Rebecca's teacher, I couldn't do this right now. I'm working hard to put my life back together after what happened in New Jersey. I'm trying to find my footing in a new place. That's enough on my plate. At least, it's as much as I can handle."

Though the day was clear and bright, his somber look cast her heart in shadow.

"*Is* it enough?" he asked her, "Is all you're really looking for *survival?* Because when I listen to you talk about your walks here, about the red rocks and the painted sky and the way the water gushes through the canyons in a rainstorm, I hear a woman who wants to really *live.*"

Mara pinched her lower lip between her teeth to ease the deeper pain of regret. "I'm sorry, Adam. I am, but I need to go back to being your daughter's Miss Stillwell, and you need to be the father so busy with his work he has to send his housekeeper to come pick up his child."

He studied her face before nodding. "All right, then. If that's what you want…Miss Stillwell."

As he turned and walked away from her, Mara stared after him and wondered how getting what she'd asked for could hurt so very much.

Her mind seething with regret and worry, Mara didn't drive straight home but instead took the scenic loop that snaked among immense, red-orange formations. Against the blue November sky, the weathered rock stood stark and steady, just as it had through thousands of human generations. As it would stand long after she and her problems had all turned to dust.

Eventually the hum of the road beneath her tires, the ancient peace of sun and sky and stone, cleared her head and carried her home two hours later. Once there, she spent a moment fumbling with the deadbolt Enrique had installed that morning, along with safety latches designed to allow the kitchen window to be raised no higher than the half-inch needed to allow the orange power cord snaking through from the generator outside.

Not an ideal situation, but she could live with it until Monday, presuming Adam still meant to send the work crew to replace the fuse box after she'd told him she wanted a strictly professional relationship. But no sooner had the thought occurred than she dismissed it. *It's not in that man to break his promise*. It was one of the things she loved about him.

Loved? She shook her head at her own foolishness and fought to banish the memory of the way his mouth had tasted, the way he'd felt, so hard against her.

Groaning in frustration, she put her purse down and got herself an ice-cold glass of water from the fridge. Jasper burst out of the bedroom mewing, and she fed him before remembering she needed to recharge her cell phone.

Pulling it from her bag, she saw she had a voice mail, though whoever left it had blocked the caller ID.

Mara's stomach spasmed at the thought that it might be Mrs. Rhodes, wanting to dismiss her. Or Barbara Fairmont playing "Harper Valley hypocrite" to shame a sinner. Or could it be Adam, wanting to meet with Mara to discuss things? She felt a traitorous flutter of excitement at where that possibility might lead.

She played the message, and at first she thought it was her brother calling from Afghanistan, his voice garbled by a bad connection. But as her brain untangled meaning from the distorted words, all thoughts of Trace vanished.

"Her head shattered," the message began. *"Skull smashed like a pumpkin when it hit the rocks. Leave now, little teacher. Get out of here and live."*

Trembling overtook her, gorge rising hot as she held the phone at arm's length. Who would…? What kind of sick person…? In her shock, she couldn't finish a coherent thought. Instead, she stood frozen for what seemed like an eternity before she managed to convince herself she'd surely heard wrong, her brain constructing a vile threat from the background static and warped voice.

She replayed the message once, twice, and finally a third time, in an attempt to move beyond shock and revulsion. The voice itself was no help, so distorted Mara couldn't even be certain whether it was male or female.

But she had her suspicions. Suspicions about Barbara Fairmont and even Jillian Rhodes, though it was ridiculous to think of a respected principal doing something as insane as leaving a veiled death threat on a teacher's voice mail.

Mara frowned, recalling the pry marks on her front door, indicating that someone had recently tried to force it open. Feeling sick, she realized that whatever was going on here could be deadly serious. Far too serious to handle on her own.

Call Adam, she thought, forgetting that she should be thinking of him as a student's father and not a personal friend. But then she dismissed the idea. The reference to Adam's late wife on the message, the implication that the caller might have witnessed Christine Jakes' death, was so horrifying, she couldn't fathom allowing him to hear it.

Besides, she had been horribly wrong about a man once, not so long ago. Though instinct and intuition screamed against it, could she risk even the smallest chance that she was wrong about Adam, too? That a seemingly caring man could somehow have been involved with…?

Nearly choking on the thought, she grabbed the land line and dialed 9-1-1.

His heart pounding, Adam clutched the phone, then raced from his home office to find Mrs. Somers in the kitchen with Rebecca. His daughter looked up from the book report cover she was decorating.

"Daddy?" she asked, her pale eyes worried. As sensitive as she was, she clearly read the state of his emotions.

He fought to mask his unease, to hide it from his child. Manufacturing a safe lie, he said, "I have to go out, honey. Little problem at the building site."

With an apron encircling her trim form, Mrs. Somers peered at him over the half glasses she'd been using to read a recipe. "No one hurt, I hope? You look a little shaken."

"Nothing like that," he said. "But I may be gone for a few hours."

He prayed he wasn't lying, that Mara hadn't been hurt. But Enrique hadn't known, had told him only that the sheriff himself had just strode past the main house and knocked at Mara's door.

"I knew you'd want to know, amigo," Enrique had told him. "Considering the way you feel about *la maestra*. And because it's *him* that's with her."

By *him,* Enrique meant Ronnie Rayburn, the sheriff Adam—and half the town—knew had been carrying on with Christine in the months before her death. Though married himself, Rayburn was well-known for his womanizing, and he made no secret of his preference for lonely housewives.

As Adam hurried to his car, he felt his hands curl into fists at the thought of the man who had seen Christine's unhappiness and slipped in to take advantage. The man who'd left her feeling emptier than ever, weeping as she'd begged Adam for forgiveness for straying.

The man who'd been so quick to rule his wife's death accidental. Suspicious, Adam had hired private detectives to look into the matter, but so far, they'd found nothing.

Nothing except reasons why his wife, who'd struggled for years with clinical depression, might have harmed herself.

But he reminded himself that today wasn't about Christine but a woman who was still alive, a woman he was still able to help. And he was damned well going to help Mara, whether she wanted it or not.

Chapter 5

"I'm real sorry somebody's had the poor taste to play such a cruel prank." Tall and powerfully built, with strong cheekbones and a square jaw, Sheriff Rayburn removed his hat, revealing close-cropped, sandy hair tipped silver at the temples. Though Mara wouldn't exactly call him handsome, his sorrowful hazel gaze and total focus held an undeniable appeal.

But Mara wasn't interested. Above the generator's hum, she said, "A prank? You think this is a joke? With what this person said about how Christine Jakes died?"

Rayburn's color deepened, and his eyes grew more intent. "What do you know about Christine Jakes?"

"I teach the poor woman's daughter, so of course I've heard about her accident."

Relaxing visibly, he nodded.

"And I know Adam." Mara scooped up her kitten to keep him from sharpening his claws on Rayburn's pant leg. "He was a high school friend of my brother's, back in New Jersey."

Rayburn asked her a few more questions about her "history"

with the Jakes family and any enemies she might have. As much as she hated to bring up the possibility, Mara said, "There *was* a squabble with one of the parents at the school. She's the PTO president."

"Who?"

"Well, I'm sure it couldn't be her, but…Barbara Fairmont."

Head shaking, Rayburn chuckled. "Not her style, believe me. I have to figure this is some idiot's idea of a sick joke. Maybe an applicant who wanted the job you got, but more likely somebody out to stir up trouble for Mr. Jakes."

"Who would want to do that? From what I've heard, everyone around here is excited about the new resort."

"Mover and shaker like Jakes, he rubs some folks the wrong way." Rayburn's tone implied he might be one of those people. "Besides, when it comes to a big-money project like he's building, there's always some fellow on the outside who wishes he was in."

"But if someone's mad at him, why come after me?"

"Maybe this person thinks it'd be easier to hurt Jakes through someone he might care for rather than try and get to him personally. Pretty cowardly, you ask me." Rayburn thoughtfully rubbed his chin. "Yeah, the way I figure this, it's nothing to do with you, miss. Nothing personal, I mean."

"I have to tell you, Sheriff, I *do* take death threats personally. And what about these pry marks?" Mara opened the door to point them out again. "The ones nobody from your office called me back about. Those seem pretty personal to me, too."

He shrugged. "Wish I could tell you we don't have the occasional B&E around here. But I see you've got yourself a stout lock now. How about your window latches?"

"They were replaced, too."

He reached out to rub the kitten's ear—only to pull away when Jasper took a swipe at him and hissed. "Whoa! Well, with all that and this vicious guard cat on duty, I'd say you've got the bases covered." Rayburn smiled and winked as he slipped her his card. "But if you have any other troubles, Mara, you be sure and call me. My cell and home numbers are written on the back."

Was this guy serious? "What about the message? Don't you want a copy for evidence or something?"

"Well, I guess I could do that," he said. "Who's your cell phone provider? I'll see if they can trace the caller."

Though she had the impression he was humoring her, she gave him the information. Not that she'd been expecting him to get on the phone with Quantico and demand a voiceprint analysis.

"Remember, you need anything, even a friendly tour of Red Bluff, be sure and call me. Day or night." With another wink, he tipped his hat to her before leaving.

She was still staring after him, realizing she had just been hit on, when she caught sight of Adam striding toward them, both men on a collision course.

Some thirty yards distant, Mara saw the tension in their bodies, like the circling of two wolves with their hackles raised. They didn't shake hands—didn't say much, either—before Rayburn stormed off toward his patrol car and Adam headed her way, strain written on his face.

"Enrique called me. What happened?" he asked.

Mara shook her head. "I think I just met the smarmy version of Andy Griffith."

Adam didn't smile.

"You're okay, aren't you? No one's hurt you?" His gaze searched her, his need for reassurance palpable. "Did someone get inside this time?"

"I'm fine," she assured him. "Just a little prank, that's all. I overreacted."

"What kind of prank?"

"An anonymous phone call suggesting I might like to leave

town." No way would she share the caller's cruel words about his wife's death.

"Barbara Fairmont," he growled. "The woman's a menace. But don't worry. I promise you, I *will* straighten her out."

"No, Adam. We've been through this." Mara locked on to his gaze. "It's my problem to deal with. She's had it in for me from day one, mostly because I won't let her son hurt the other children."

"You're just doing your job, and I intend to make sure—"

"I *intend* to take care of it myself, or no one in this community will ever take me seriously. Besides…" Mara gentled her voice. "You're just another parent now, remember? At least until the school year's over."

She allowed herself the barest smile.

Adam searched her eyes. "So you're telling me if I back off now, there could be a later?"

Her heartbeat fluttering, she managed, "Starting on June sixth. *If* we're both still interested."

"You can count on it, Miss Stillwell." A smile warmed his handsome features. "And you can be certain, too, I'll be watching from the sidelines, making sure you're safe."

"Sidelines it is," she said lightly.

"Until midnight, Mara. Midnight on June sixth." With a smoldering look, he turned and left her.

Left her to a very restless night.

A cold front came in early Sunday, casting a threatening gray pall over Red Bluff. Tucked beneath her blankets, Mara barely noticed the chill until her cell phone rang and she jolted upright, stomach lurching at the memory of the message she'd received the day before.

She peered at the caller ID window, her stomach flipping all over again when she saw the name *Rhodes*. If the principal was calling, Babzilla must have been as good as her initial threat.

"Good morning." Mara fought to keep her voice steady, as if this were any other Sunday and she had no idea what was coming.

"I trust you're feeling better." Mrs. Rhodes' voice sounded strained, her "concern" superficial.

"Much," said Mara. *At least until you called.*

"Glad to hear it, Miss Stillwell, because I need you to come immediately. We have a situation at the school." Anger frosted the words with brittle ice.

"A situation?"

"Meet me in your classroom and we'll discuss it face-to-face."

"I'll be there in half an hour."

"I'll expect you in twenty minutes," Mrs. Rhodes warned.

Mara dressed hurriedly, brushed her teeth and pulled her hair back before forcing herself to slow down. *You can't defend yourself if you rush in flustered.*

She drove carefully, drawing what small comfort she could from the way the low clouds broke like the sea against the red rocks. But the scenic beauty didn't help as she pulled in to the school's lot, where a pair of sheriff's department patrol cars flanked Jillian Rhodes' sedan.

What on earth? Surely, Mrs. Rhodes hadn't called the authorities about her. Mara hopped out of her car, then walked briskly through the unlocked front breezeway gate and back to her classroom, where the door stood wide open. Mrs. Rhodes, dressed impeccably as always, stood with her arms crossed, speaking with a deputy who was writing something on a clipboard he had balanced on a bowling ball–size belly.

As Mara reached them, heart in throat, she spotted the other deputy inside the classroom. Then she got her first glimpse of the damage. "What happened?"

"District security spotted the back gate open." Mrs. Rhodes pointed out a line of red footprints on the sidewalk. Footprints leading from her classroom door. "And then this."

Moving to the doorway, Mara saw the red paint—it must have been gallons—splashed across the walls like blood, coagulating on the desktops and soaked into the carpet. Computers had been smashed to pieces, from the one on her desk to the five student work stations along the back counter. The drawers of her desk had been pulled out and emptied, along with her supply cabinets and bookshelves. Papers were strewn everywhere, most speckled by or sticking to the paint.

Not here, not where children learned and worked and flourished. Her shock gave way to outrage. "How— who…?"

The second deputy, a man with leathery tanned skin and a graying mustache, emerged from the classroom holding a camera and shaking his head. "Kids, I'd say, judging from those footprints—maybe junior high age. Pack of troublemakers saw their chance when they found unlocked doors. But we'll catch 'em, don't you worry. Little punks do something this big, they tend to brag about it. Someone nearly always turns them in."

Mara was shaking her head. "But I didn't leave the door unlocked. I'd never—"

"You were here yesterday, working," Mrs. Rhodes accused, her voice stern. "And I'm told you left rather suddenly, with every reason in the world to be quite flustered."

Great. "I clearly remember locking that door. The gate, too."

"I'm sure you meant to, miss." The overweight deputy, whose nametag read J. R. Smith, sounded sympathetic. "But sometimes, when we're rushing or upset, we forget—"

"I'm absolutely positive." Mara *knew* she was right.

Mrs. Rhodes glared at her. "Do you have any idea what this is going to cost the district?"

"I'm sorry about that, but I still didn't—"

"Please, Miss Stillwell...who else am I to think did it? You were the last one here."

"No," said Mara. "Mrs. Fairmont was meeting with the carnival committee. And she has a master key, right?"

Mrs. Rhodes' brows angled sharply. "She certainly does not have access to the classrooms. And even if she did, you can't seriously be suggesting that she walked back here after the other mothers left, opened only *your* classroom door, and then unlocked the back gates before turning around and locking up the front ones?"

Mara lifted her chin. "Didn't you ask at the last faculty meeting whether anyone had seen *your* key ring?"

The radio on Deputy Smith's belt squawked, and both he and his partner stepped away to deal with it.

"They turned up the very next day," Mrs. Rhodes snapped. "And what are you implying? That a member of the staff or a parent would come here to frame you?"

"Someone trashed this room. Maybe the same person who unlocked the gate and door."

"Don't be absurd."

Suddenly, belatedly, Mara's shell-shocked brain made the connection between what had happened here and at the casita. "Yesterday I called the sheriff about a telephone threat. I had my locks upgraded, too, because someone tried to pry open my door."

Mrs. Rhodes look startled. "You've been threatened?"

"The voice was disguised, but the caller implied I would die if I didn't pack up and leave Red Bluff."

"Die?" Color draining from her face, Mrs. Rhodes glanced back at the door, where a crude obscenity stood out in runny letters. "You're saying—the sheriff *will* confirm this, won't he?"

"Here's his card." Reaching into her purse, Mara produced Rayburn's numbers. "Call him now, if you like."

"Are you aware," Mrs. Rhodes asked the deputies as they

returned, "that this vandalism could be something personal? Something directed at Miss Stillwell?"

Mara explained what she had reported. "At the time, Sheriff Rayburn didn't feel any of it was serious."

The two deputies glanced at one another. "We'll check with the sheriff, miss," said Smith, "and get back to you once we know something. But I'm afraid for right now, we have to leave you ladies. Another call's come in. More vandalism, this time over at the new resort."

"Adam Jakes' project…" said Mara.

As the men hurried away, Mrs. Rhodes took another look at the mess and sighed. "Your class will have to be relocated to the library for the time being. Perhaps it would be best if we kept on your substitute, too. Considering everything that's happened these past few days."

Mara sensed she was talking about more than the phone threat and vandalism. "I know Barbara Fairmont talked to you about what she walked in on yesterday."

"Of course she spoke to me about your…indiscretion. And I must say, I'm terribly disappointed."

"I understand, and I'm sorry. It won't happen again. I've spoken to Adam—Mr. Jakes, and we won't be spending time alone together as long as Rebecca is my student."

Over the tops of her half glasses, Mrs. Rhodes pinned Mara with a stern look. "She isn't any longer. I'm transferring her to Mrs. Kelly's classroom."

"What? Why? It's taken me months to build Rebecca's trust and foster her friendship with a couple of the other girls. If you pull her now, she'll be devastated."

"Pippa Kelly's a fine teacher. Well-grounded in the fundamentals." A pointed look underscored the final word.

"This isn't about teaching techniques, though, is it? It's about punishing me because that's what your friend wants," Mara shot back.

Mrs. Rhodes' eyes flared, her face reddening. "Barbara

Fairmont doesn't tell me how to handle my staff. It's simply clear to me that when it comes to the Jakes girl, you've lost all objectivity, and you've certainly left yourself open to charges of favoritism from the other parents."

"What other parents have complained? Aside from Mrs. Fairmont, whose child has been allowed to run amok up until this point?" Cody could be in danger, too, Mara suddenly realized, if his mother was insane enough to trash her own son's classroom.

"Miss Stillwell. Do *not* take that tone with me," the principal warned. "I won't have this behavior in my school. Understand that, as a non-tenured teacher, your contract can easily be terminated—especially considering your continual disregard for my directives."

"What?"

Mrs. Rhodes' look was withering. "You've been handing in one set of plans to keep me happy and following them only when you know I'll be in your classroom to observe."

Mara wondered how she'd figured it out.

"Did you forget the intercom in your classroom works both ways?"

"So you've been *spying* on me?"

"I only intended to confirm you were handling Cody Fairmont fairly. Knowing the boy, I suspected Barbara might be exaggerating her claims." Mrs. Rhodes shook her head. "But Cody's not the issue. It's your dishonesty."

"Did you happen to check out any of the links to educational research I shared with you? Or compare my students' reading test results to the other second graders'? The children absolutely love this technique, and Pippa's excited to try it, too." In fact, it had been Pippa's idea to win over Mrs. Rhodes by testing the two classes side by side, but Mara wasn't about to throw her new friend under the bus.

"My school is not a laboratory," Mrs. Rhodes insisted. "Nor

are our students subjects for your experimentation. This is the last time I intend to warn you."

Mara stood. "You're right. I thought my students' progress and enthusiasm would convince you, but it was a mistake to go about it the way I did. I'm sorry. I'm sorry about what happened yesterday at school, and even sorrier if anything I did resulted in that vandalism. But *don't* punish Rebecca for my mistakes. Don't hurt a child because you're upset."

"This is too much, really. Go home and stay home, Mara. At least until the next board meeting, when we'll be discussing whether your termination's the best option for everyone involved."

Chapter 6

Adam surveyed the damage: a temporary storage building with its door pried open, the construction materials inside it ruined and tools scattered. And gallons of paint missing, some of it splashed up against the windows and new adobe facing of the nearly completed five-star restaurant that was set to open within weeks. The paint was mostly dry now, indicating that this had happened sometime in the night.

"Could have been a lot worse," he told the deputies who had shown up to take the report. At least none of their expensive equipment had gone missing, and the restaurant's interior remained untouched.

"They didn't even bother smashing out the windows," he added. "If you ask me, this was kind of a halfhearted effort. All of it easily repaired." Nuisance though it was, it shouldn't put a dent in his timetable for getting the first phase of the project running.

"I don't know," said the deeply tanned Deputy Ortega. "That black paint looks pretty angry."

"Not half as angry as what we saw at our last call, sir." The heavyset Deputy Smith spoke deferentially, as he had even in those first tense days that followed Christine's death. Likely impressed by Adam's money. "Happened over at Red Bluff Elementary."

Jolted, Adam said, "That's where my daughter goes. What happened?"

"Just one classroom damaged, sir," Smith explained. "But it's a total wreck. Lots of paint there, too. Bloodred paint."

"Which classroom? Whose?"

Deputy Ortega's leathery expression hardened, the suspicion in his eyes reminding Adam of the man's pointed questions following Christine's death.

By way of explanation, Adam added, "I'm concerned that someone who's angry with me might be taking it out on my little girl. Or the woman teaching her."

"It was Mara Stillwell's classroom," Ortega allowed. "I understand she's had some other troubles, too. Too bad, a pretty young woman, new to town like that. Hardly knows a soul around here yet, I'd imagine."

His tone implied that he'd heard otherwise, or that he at least suspected she and Adam were personally entangled.

Adam explained how he'd known Mara and her brother in New Jersey. How in an effort to help his daughter work through her mother's loss, Mara had been giving Rebecca art lessons after school. "I consider Miss Stillwell a friend."

"A *close* friend?" Ortega asked, his brown eyes stony.

"I'm not sleeping with her, if that's what you're implying," Adam said bluntly.

"Meaning no offense, sir." Smith shot his partner an anxious look and tentatively suggested, "Do you think maybe someone else might've noticed you're friends and not liked it? Some guy looking to get the new schoolteacher to himself?"

"She's only lived here a few months," Adam said. "I don't think she's dated anyone here."

"Might not matter. Might just be some guy who wants to know her better. Or what about somebody from back home?" Smith continued. "Somebody who didn't want her coming out here? Who couldn't stand to let go?"

As far as Adam knew, Mara's ex-fiancé was either in jail or out on bond, awaiting trial. And she hadn't indicated he might still be a problem. "You should certainly ask her, but I don't know of anybody like that from her past."

"What about you, Mr. Jakes? Anybody with a grudge you're aware of? A business partner you cut out of all this?" Ortega gestured from the defaced restaurant to the huge lodge and guest casitas, still under construction. With a sneer in his voice, he added, "Or maybe you have some unhappy investors?"

"I don't cheat my associates." The ice in Adam's voice was sharp enough to cut. "And I don't mislead my investors."

"We didn't mean anything by it," Smith added quickly.

Ortega's gaze said otherwise. "Have you received any anonymous calls or letters, any threats or warnings?"

Adam shook his head. "Nothing."

"What about unusual attempts to solicit 'donations'?" Beneath the lowering sky, Smith was sweating in the chilly air, perspiration beading his upper lip.

"Nothing like that, either."

"There's always blackmail," Ortega said pointedly. "Someone claiming to know secrets—the kinds of secrets that can land even a rich man in hot water."

Adam swore, then challenged, "You want to accuse me of something, Deputy? Then do it. But unless you have hard evidence, I wouldn't advise standing around here slinging innuendo about crimes that haven't been committed. Not when you have several real ones you need to get busy solving."

It took several moments for Ortega to collect himself to answer. "Sorry if you were offended. Just trying to cover all the bases."

Adam didn't buy the deputy's supposed contrition. Whether

he suspected Adam of a crime or resented his wealth and position, Ortega clearly didn't like him.

"If you're busy," Smith said soothingly, "we'll talk to your construction supervisor, have him accompany us while we finish our evidence collection."

"I think that would be a fine idea," Adam told them. "It seems I have other matters to attend to."

As Mara drove back home, the rain set in, a cold, gray downpour that cascaded off rock and hard-packed soil, and filled the arroyos, normally dry channels that crisscrossed the area.

"Great," she muttered, realizing she had no umbrella. But why shouldn't the sky dump on her? With her classroom trashed and Jillian Rhodes bent on her dismissal, getting soaked was just par for the course.

Mara wished she'd never come to this two-stoplight town. Wished she'd dug in her heels and faced her problems on her home turf. But the fact remained, Red Bluff was the only home she had left—one she couldn't afford, emotionally or financially, to lose.

Which meant that, tempting as it was, self-pity was no option, and neither was blind panic. She needed to keep her wits about her, to call the teachers' union representative and see if they would provide a lawyer to help get her through this.

But what she really wanted now was someone who cared for her. Someone who wouldn't judge, who would simply be there. Maybe Pippa, she thought. Pippa would be kind.

No sooner had the idea occurred than Mara dismissed it. She didn't want Pippa's sympathy; she wanted Adam, with his arms around her. Adam, who would be outraged on her behalf.

Not a good idea, she knew. For one thing, she would end up fighting to keep him from marching straight to Jillian Rhodes' home and lighting into the principal with a blistering attack. For another, she absolutely knew that if he came over, they would end up in bed together, which would only complicate the situation further.

She tamped down the thought, even though it made her ache with frustration.

With a sigh, she turned into the Trejos' empty driveway and nudged her Mini beneath the open carport. After tucking her things inside a plastic grocery sack, she dashed for the front door. Soaked before she reached it, she fumbled with the new lock before remembering she'd shut off the generator to save fuel before she'd left.

Wet as she was, she ran back outside to restart it so she would have lights and could run her electric heater, not to mention her refrigerator. After returning in record time and dashing inside, she shivered through the act of changing into dry jeans and her warmest sweatshirt. With the rain beating against the roof, she dried her hair and, yawning, grabbed a throw off her bed.

It might be only noon, but she was bone tired, wrung out by the destruction of her classroom, the confrontation with her principal, and the crush of emotions falling as thick around her as the driving rain outside.

She lay back with her head aching, wondering if the stress of the past two days had triggered a relapse into illness. She would call the union rep later—and Pippa, too—she decided, putting off the inevitable.

Minutes later, she popped up. Where was Jasper? Normally the kitten charged out to attack her shoelaces or beg a treat or a chin-scratch whenever she came inside.

Rising to wander through the four small rooms, she called him. When he didn't come, she took out his box of kitten food and shook it. No response, but tiny as the little guy was, there were any number of places he might hide.

More than likely scared of the rain's noise, she thought.

Poor thing had never heard it before, probably thought the world was coming to an end.

Better to let him come out on his own than frighten him further by tearing apart the place to find him. Besides, her head was pounding now, and she felt slightly dizzy. She wanted nothing more than to sit down.

Irritated with herself, she struggled to fight off her lethargy. In a fit of pique, she went to her little kitchen table and dumped the papers she'd brought home to grade.

Attending to them, she told herself, was an act of faith. A compact between herself and the students she swore she would return to teach.

But as she reached for one paper that had sailed onto the floor, she froze, the events of the past two days instantly banished from her mind.

It was a drawing, a piece of child's artwork immediately recognizable as Rebecca's. Another of her "falling" pictures, this one, too, depicted a figure pitching forward from a bluff's edge.

Except in this picture, the mouth — clearly female—formed a red O of horror, and another person's hands were visible at the paper's edge.

The hands that had pushed Christine Jakes to her death, Mara realized, a sick chill ripping through her body. Monstrous, claw-tipped hands that made a mockery of the sheriff's ruling of accidental death or any of the rumors suggesting suicide.

Rebecca Jakes was telling Mara, in the only way she could, that her mother had been murdered. And whatever the girl knew, it was coming clearer all the time.

I have to call Adam, Mara thought. *I have to talk to him about this.*

But by that time the throbbing in her head was so insistent that the mere thought of speaking left her nauseated. Migraine, she realized, reminded of past episodes—and the medicine she carried in her purse just in case. After taking her pill, she lay back against the sofa's cushions and closed her eyes in the hope she would soon feel better.

Her last coherent thought was that this felt different from a normal migraine. Different enough that instead of taking her pill, she should have called someone for help.

Chapter 7

The torrent sheeted off rocky soil and cascaded down the streets surrounding Red Bluff, including the steep and winding road leading to Adam's construction project.

Faced with dangerous driving conditions, he stopped at home, rather than making the treacherous journey to ask Mara about the situation at the school. He would call her instead, he decided, or at least wait until the weather improved.

But the moment he entered through the attached garage, he heard his daughter crying. Not the quiet snuffles he'd seen from time to time since her mother's death, but sobs so hard she sounded breathless.

Certain she'd been hurt, he raced toward the crying, which led to his home office. Just outside the doorway, he found Mrs. Somers on her knees, her arms wrapped around Rebecca, who was struggling to pull away, her face red.

"What's wrong? What happened?" Kneeling beside her, Adam scanned for blood, protruding bones, anything to explain the noise. *"Rebecca?"*

She turned to stare, her damp blue eyes astonished, since he so rarely raised his voice around her. But the shock lasted only moments before her lower lip began to wobble. "They're—they're going to make me change teachers. They're taking me out of Miss Stillwell's class!"

"What? Who told you such a thing?" Adam asked, furious to imagine that his own thoughtless behavior—that ill-timed kiss with Mara—might have sparked such a disaster.

Rebecca pointed at the phone on his desk, and Mrs. Somers nodded to confirm it.

The housekeeper stood, knees cracking, and rubbed the small of her back. "Rebecca went to get some printer paper from your office for another picture, and your answering machine was taking a message. I didn't hear it myself, but apparently—"

"It was the principal," Rebecca said, still crying. "Was I bad? Is that why she's changing me to Mrs. Kelly's room?"

As Adam hugged his daughter, he felt the pounding of her heart. Hadn't this poor kid been through enough? "Nobody's changing anybody, sweetie. Let me have a little privacy so I can sort out this mistake."

Rebecca pulled away to look up at him. "It's a mistake, that's all? And you can fix it?"

"I'll do my very best. But you know what? It's really getting cold out. I would love a big mug of hot chocolate. Do you think you could help Mrs. Somers make the good kind?"

Over the girl's head, his gaze met the housekeeper's. Mrs. Somers nodded and said, "Come along, Rebecca. You can help me measure out the cocoa."

Once they were gone, he closed the office door and listened to the message, a tense-sounding Jillian Rhodes explaining that she felt it was "in everyone's best interest" to transfer Rebecca to Mrs. Kelly's class beginning Monday. She'd left her home number, too, "should you like to discuss this further."

"You'd better believe I'd like to discuss it." Adam stabbed at the numbers he'd just taken down, then stood facing the window, the rain outside so heavy, his expensive view dissolved into a silver haze.

"This is Jillian Rhodes," she answered on the first ring. "I was expecting your call, Mr. Jakes."

"What on earth is going on?" he demanded. "My daughter heard your message, and now she's in hysterics. She absolutely loves Miss Stillwell."

"I'm sorry to hear that," Mrs. Rhodes said. "Unfortunately, this change is necessary, for everyone involved."

"I heard there was a break-in. Some damage to Miss Stillwell's classroom." Outside, the wind shifted, driving the water against the window. Adam moved away from it to hear.

"Extensive damage," Mrs. Rhodes corrected. "And I understand you had an incident today, as well. At your work-site."

"Nothing major. Just a little paint damage and some easily replaceable supplies."

"Considering what Miss Stillwell told me about a phone threat and attempted break-in at her home, I'm guessing that someone's taken notice of what's going on between the two of you. Which, I must say, is entirely inappropriate. Especially with what I'm told happened in the classroom."

"I didn't call you to be scolded like a second grader," he said. "I called to keep you from taking out what happened, *after school hours,* on a seven-year-old."

"This isn't about punishing Rebecca," Mrs. Rhodes insisted. "I mean to keep her safe from whoever's doing such dreadful things. Besides, it's a conflict of interest for Miss Stillwell to be—"

"I'm completely capable of seeing to my daughter's safety, and Miss Stillwell and I have agreed to keep our distance."

"As far as I'm concerned, you're welcome to work out the

details of your private lives between yourselves—with Rebecca in Mrs. Kelly's class. I'll explain to your daughter—"

"No, that's not acceptable. Rebecca's flourishing this year. I was at my wits' end, but now she's talking, loving school again, catching up to where she should be with her work. You know how bad she was all last year. This is a child's mental health we're talking about."

"I'm well versed in children's mental health, Mr. Jakes. And I'm afraid this is an area where the principal has discretion."

"I *believe* the superintendent has the discretion to overrule you." Adam let the comment hang, giving Mrs. Rhodes a chance to reflect upon the superintendent's enthusiasm for the increased tax revenues that would result from Adam's project. Already, the district had planning committees discussing the construction of a newer, larger elementary school and an addition for the high school.

Normally Adam would have bent over backward to avoid looking as if he was throwing around his money and influence, but he wasn't risking his daughter's emotional well-being.

"Rebecca's teacher will be Mara Stillwell," he told the principal flatly.

"I'm afraid that Mara Stillwell," Mrs. Rhodes said irritably, "won't be teaching anyone's children for the time being."

"What are you talking about?" Worry undercut him, dropping him into his chair. "Mara's not hurt, is she? Has something—did someone…?"

"She's fine, as far as that goes."

"So this is a disciplinary matter?" he asked.

"I'm afraid I'm legally barred from discussing personnel issues. As is the superintendent." Her tone told Adam that she resented his bringing up her boss. "I'm afraid you'll have to wait until next month's school board meeting to present your concerns."

"Forget it," he said sharply. "I'll find out what's going on myself. But no matter what, you can count on one thing. My daughter's absolutely not going to be in another teacher's class tomorrow. I'll pull her out of your school before I allow it."

"Shall I have the paperwork drawn up?" Mrs. Rhodes asked lightly.

Too angry to answer without saying something he would likely regret later, Adam slammed down the receiver and grabbed the local phone book. Because one way or another, he was going to get answers.

Sound drilled through Mara's thoughts. A sound that had her reaching for her cell phone before its ringing registered. But rather than grabbing it to answer, her clumsy movement sent it spinning off the coffee table and landing out of reach.

She meant to sit up. Meant to reach down to pick it up. But the first movement of her head slammed her with pain that started at her right eye and arced over her skull. Pain of a migraine so intense that bile rose to meet it. Why hadn't her medicine worked this time?

By going still, she managed to keep from vomiting, but it was a near thing, an exhausting effort. By that time the phone had stopped its ringing, the torturous noise that drilled into her head. She wished she could turn off the angry hiss of the rain, too, the snare-drum beat of drops driven like nails into her brain.

Just sleep it off, she thought. Sleep would set this pain right. And on some level, as she drifted, she dared imagine it would solve her other problems, too.

With Enrique assuring him that Mara's car was parked where it belonged, Adam was sure she had to be there. Probably too upset to answer his call, or maybe she'd decided he had already caused her enough trouble.

Sipping at his hot chocolate, he weighed that possibility

against the idea that she might need him. Weighed his "tendency toward overprotectiveness," which the family counselor had called an understandable reaction to Christine's death, against the knowledge that Mara wasn't his to care for.

Not unless I make her mine, some misbegotten instinct whispered.

And that was never going to happen if he let Jillian Rhodes and Barbara Fairmont run Mara out of Red Bluff. His mind made up, he went to tell Mrs. Somers he had to drive to town.

"In this?" Worry in her gray eyes, she gestured toward the kitchen window. Though she was no more than fifteen years his senior, there were times when she acted much like the mother he had lost. "Why would you risk—"

"Don't worry. I'll take the four-wheel drive," he said, referring to the black Mercedes SUV parked beside his Jaguar in the garage. Christine had insisted they buy it for those few days each winter when ice glazed the steep roads.

Since she'd mainly been the one to drive it, he'd barely touched it since her death. Mrs. Somers, too, avoided it, preferring her stalwart old Volvo.

"Are you going to see Mrs. Rhodes?" Rebecca came into the room, her eyes red and swollen. Anxiety thinned her voice as she asked, "Are you going to make sure I stay in the right class?"

Don't promise, he warned himself, hating the thought that he might disappoint her. But the hope and faith in her expression broke down his defenses, and he hugged her tight against him, a wild plan forming in his mind. A plan that would keep Rebecca happy and Mara safe, if only he could talk her into it.

"Don't you worry. I'll take care of everything," he swore.

By the time he reached town, the deluge had slackened enough that he didn't even bother grabbing an umbrella as he pulled in to the driveway behind Mara's car. Feeling anxious, since she hadn't answered two more attempts to call her, he leaped out of the Mercedes and passed through the unlocked gate.

With the generator humming outside and a light visible from within, he decided he'd guessed right about her being home. But she didn't answer, no matter how hard he pounded at her door.

"Mara!" he called. "I'm not leaving until we talk."

The only answer was a faint mewling. Looking around, he spotted Mara's kitten shivering beneath a concrete bench. Sodden to the bone, the gray-and-white creature looked miserable as Adam bent to scoop him up.

"How'd you get out, little fellow?" As fond as Mara was of the kitten, it seemed inconceivable that she would intentionally leave him out in such a storm. Adam zipped the sodden, half-frozen animal inside his jacket to warm him, then pounded at the door again.

More worried than ever by the lack of a response, he headed for the front window and cupped his hands to look inside. It was tough seeing past the blinds, but he made out something.... Was that Mara's foot there on the sofa, so still she might be...?

No! Breath freezing, he rapped hard at the glass—sucking in a lungful of air when her foot twitched at the noise. Beyond that, neither his shouting nor his pounding moved her, alarming him enough to try the door. Finding it locked, he grabbed a fist-sized rock from the garden and smashed it through the window glass.

As he reached through the hole to unlatch the window, he felt the kitten's needle-sharp claws dig into his skin. Heedless of the pain—and the jagged glass that bit deep into his wrist—he raised the window, his blood splattering the sill as he climbed inside the guesthouse.

In spite of the noise, Mara barely stirred. Kneeling by the

sofa, Adam scanned her for injuries. Seeing none, he shook her, saying, "Mara, time to wake up."

She didn't respond.

His head started pounding, his vision swimming out of focus, as he pulled out his phone and dialed 9-1-1. After giving the address, he said, "Unconscious woman in the back, in the casita, and I'm…"

He fumbled, dropping his phone to land not far from Mara's.…

And suddenly, he knew. What had happened to her was happening to him, too. And it would kill them both if he didn't get them out into the fresh air.

With no time for finesse, he grabbed Mara and slung her over his shoulder. Though normally he would have had no problem carrying her light frame, he staggered, the door seeming to pull away from his approach.

The room dimmed, and the horizon tilted. But the frightened kitten inside his jacket squirmed, its needle-sharp claws rousing Adam long enough to fling open the casita's door and lurch through it into the misting rain.

He barely made it another two steps before he went down hard on his knees, dropping Mara as he joined her in unconsciousness.

Chapter 8

Bright, Mara realized dimly. Everything here was bright white.

Must be dreaming, she thought. Dreaming she was floating inside a cloud.

But in dreams, her mouth had never felt so dry, her stomach quite so queasy. And that noise…that wasn't the rain—or the generator, either.

Turning her head, she felt…something. Reaching up, she touched hard plastic banded to her face, and her eyes shot open.

"Hang on."

The voice was male and familiar, though she couldn't place it, and her vision refused to focus.

"Don't pull that off." He caught her hand in his and squeezed it. "You need the oxygen."

Adam… Even more than his voice, his touch gave him away.

"Oxygen?" Her question came out muffled, little more than a low moan.

"Mara." He squeezed her hand. "You could have—you nearly died in there."

His face came into focus, worry lining his forehead. Leaning forward, he pressed his lips to her temple, a touch of warmth that somehow made her shiver.

She didn't understand. How had she gotten here, in what had to be a *hospital,* with the beeping monitor beside her, the hissing oxygen and monochromatic walls?

"I have to tell the nurse you're awake so she can page the doctor," he said.

Before she could respond, he rushed out, only to return a minute later. "Someone'll be right in."

"What happened?" Mara asked.

"Carbon monoxide from the generator. Small as your place is, it built up fast."

She tapped her own wrist, then looked pointedly at the bandages on his.

"Oh, that? A little cut from breaking in to get you. It's fine."

She saw a small adhesive bandage on his forehead, too, but when she pointed to it, he shook his head and added, "Forget me. How are *you?*"

Confused, mostly, she thought. "How did you know…? I was at home, right?" She reached for the mask again.

"Leave that alone. I understood you. I got a call from Mrs. Rhodes. When she said you wouldn't be teaching—" He shook his head in disgust. "I didn't get the details, but I knew I had to check on you. And when I found your kitten out in the rain…"

"Jasper?" How could he have gotten outside? Unless Adam hadn't been her first visitor that day?

"I banged on the door, but you didn't answer, and then I saw you lying on the sofa, so still I thought—" Distress passed like a black cloud behind his eyes. "That's when I broke in. When I was nearly overcome myself, I figured it out."

Sickened, she could do no more than stare as the door opened to the nurse, who came over to check her vitals.

The doctor appeared next, an older man with kind eyes who checked her neurological responses and blood oxygen level before removing her mask and shutting off the machines.

"You're one very lucky young woman to be alive, and with all your cognitive functions intact," he said. "Carbon monoxide's a silent killer. People don't smell or feel it—they just lose consciousness and die."

Once the doctor left, Mara reached for the glass of water by her bedside, and Adam bent the straw and helped her drink.

Gentle as he was with her, anger rumbled through his voice. "I sent my best men out to set up that generator. Guys I'd trust with my life. There's no way they would've made an amateur mistake like accidentally venting the exhaust indoors."

The door swung open, and Sheriff Rayburn came in, his hat in hand and his expression grave. "Well somebody did," he said, "and there was no 'accidentally' about it. Someone clearly wanted this young lady dead."

"Who?" Adam demanded.

Rayburn gave him a sharp look. "We're working round the clock on this one. So there's no need to send in your damned private detectives to muck up my investigation."

"You do your job and find this person," Adam warned him, "and I won't *have to* do it for you."

"I'm not kidding, Adam." As she sat beside him in the Mercedes later, Mara's cheeks flamed and her green eyes narrowed. "This is a really bad idea."

He shook his head and took the turn leading to the outer rim of the mesa, where he had built his home. "Please, Mara, stop. I spoke with your brother, and we both agreed that staying in my guest quarters is the safest option."

"What is this, the Middle Ages? You honestly think you

two can decide to lock me in your castle keep like some witless damsel?"

He couldn't help smiling at the picture she had painted. "It's hardly a castle, and no one's calling anybody witless. But the doctor said you needed to be watched for problems with your memory and your motor skills, and—"

"I'm fine, and you know it. Or you ought to. You've been watching me like a hawk."

"You think that might have something to do with, oh, I don't know, someone trying to *murder you?*" He reminded himself it wasn't Mara who had angered him and added, "Trying to hurt you because of *me.* I know about the phone call, Mara. Finally dragged it out of that jackass, Rayburn. Why was it I had to hear it from him?"

"What's your problem with the sheriff, anyway?" she asked. "Every time the two of you are anywhere near each other, clouds of testosterone fill the air. Which, in the course of history, has killed more brain cells than carbon monoxide ever dreamed of."

Ignoring her attempt to distract him, Adam scowled. "Why didn't you tell me what the caller said about Christine's death?"

Mara looked down at her folded hands. "I'm sorry. I just—I couldn't. It was so…so shocking, so ugly, I thought it had to be a lie. I figured the caller was just some mean, spiteful sicko who takes pleasure from inflicting pain."

She didn't mention the moment's doubt of Adam she'd felt, doubt of the man who'd since risked his safety and even his life saving hers.

He pulled to the side of the steep road, which overlooked a trio of rock formations that shone bloodred in the crisp sunshine. Keeping his gaze locked on them, he put the SUV in Park. "*You* wanted to protect *me?*"

"I did," she admitted. "And I thought I did the right thing, turning it over to the sheriff. Are you angry with me?"

"No, of course not." He reached for her hand, brought it to his mouth and pressed his lips to it. Throat tightening, he turned toward her. "But if there's any chance this incident could be connected to my wife's death, then Ronnie Rayburn's the last person I'd trust to investigate."

"Why is that? Help me understand."

Adam told her all of it, from Christine's depression, the buildup of dissatisfaction after they had moved here—a decision she'd initially supported—and her crushing guilt when she'd admitted she'd broken her marriage vows. "With *Rayburn,* I heard later, and he's never once denied it."

"I'm so sorry. That can't have been an easy thing to hear."

He shook his head, hating the memory, the pain that struck sledgehammer hard. "Water under the bridge now. But maybe you can understand why I hired my own investigators to look into her death. Something the sheriff took as a personal insult. Not to mention the fact that I organized a fundraiser for his political opponent. He lost in the primaries last spring, but I can tell you, Rayburn won't forget I helped the guy. Not in a million years."

"Are you saying you think the sheriff has something to do with all this?"

Adam heard her skepticism, her reluctance to believe the worst of others, in spite of how badly she'd been hurt by her own fiancé's deception. But he was grateful she retained even a little of her innocence. Otherwise, she might suspect him of his wife's death, as so many others still did.

"I can't be sure of anything," he said, "except that I can't stand the thought of losing another woman that I've come to care for. I *won't,* Mara."

She leaned toward him, and when he bridged the distance, she kissed him. So softly and sweetly, the tension knotted in him eased.

"You aren't going to lose me." She touched his cheek

to assure him. "Not unless you hold on so tight I can't breathe."

An image flashed through his mind, a raw vision of himself lying prone atop the bluff and holding Christine's wrist to keep her from falling. He wished uselessly he really had been with her, that he had held on to both the woman and their troubled marriage with every ounce of his strength.

"I can't take the risk." As he looked into Mara's face, he fought to control the sharpness in his own voice. "We both know you can't go back to your casita."

"Pippa's offered me a sofa till I can resolve this situation with Mrs. Rhodes and look for a new place."

"A sofa? You'll have a well-furnished private suite at my house, for as long as you need it."

"I appreciate the thought," she said carefully, "but if I move in with you, in the middle of the school year, it's going to look to everyone as if we're—"

"The guest suite is basically its own apartment inside the house," he said. "It's totally self-contained."

"You can't seriously think that's going to stop the Barbara Fairmonts of this town from talking, or the school board from—"

"Forget them. Work for *me,* Mara, not the district. Teach the way you want to, the way that's working so well for Rebecca. Because I'll be damned if I'll let anybody take away the best thing that's happened to my daughter in…"

Ever, he wanted to say, thinking of Christine's pervasive sadness, her frequent tears and self-recrimination. Long before she'd died, she'd stopped being not only the wife he yearned for but the mother Rebecca needed. The mother his sweet and blameless child deserved.

"That's very generous of you, Adam. But I'm a teacher, not some rich man's governess. And it especially wouldn't be appropriate when I—when both of us have feelings…"

Her lips pursed, making him want to kiss her hard. To take her home and to bed, banishing her every objection.

Which probably wouldn't be the best way to convince her that he wasn't making the offer out of lust or even a need to protect her, but for Rebecca's sake. To prevent himself from touching her, he put the SUV into gear and pulled back onto the road.

"We can keep this strictly professional," he assured her.

She smiled and shook her head. "No matter what Mrs. Rhodes says, I'm going to keep my job at Red Bluff. Rebecca can be in my class then. Now turn around, please, and take me to Pippa's."

"At least come and say hello to Rebecca. She's been terribly worried—"

"You didn't *tell* her, did you?"

"I explained you had a small accident," Adam said, "but it was hard to hide my worry from her."

"She's very sensitive, very intuitive about others' feelings. I've seen that in the classroom."

"She's also been very diligent about taking care of Jasper."

"Thank you for that, Adam, and yes, I'll go with you to thank her and let her see for herself that I'm okay. But don't even think of using that little girl to maneuver me into staying. Because I'm absolutely, positively, not going to be the live-in help."

Minutes later, Mara sucked in a deep breath as they rounded a curve that revealed the grand home high above them, an adobe masterpiece whose color blended into the stark red bluffs around it. Save for the sharp-edged shadows and the sun's gleam off the windows, her eye might have passed over it completely.

But when the automatic gates slid open to allow them entrance, the mansion's size and simple grandeur fully hit her. "You built this…" she breathed, understanding at once why he'd once told her that he remained an architect at heart, though the scope of his business had gone far beyond that.

"I had a bit of help," he said modestly, but she saw fierce pride in his expression, pride tempered by the sadness of the tragedy that had taken place so nearby. A tragedy that had marked him as much as it had Rebecca.

Abruptly, the girl's last picture, the one Mara had been looking at just before the gas had overwhelmed her, flashed through her mind. The screaming face, the outstretched arms, the bluff whose horrifyingly familiar silhouette she'd noticed just before they pulled into the gates.

Along with the memory came her suspicion that Rebecca had seen something. That the child had been a witness to her mother's murder.

"It's a gorgeous home," Mara forced herself to say, rather than bring up what she was really thinking about. Not to mention that it occurred to her that Rebecca might be drawing nightmares or dark imaginings. To discuss the subject would be too cruel—not until she knew for sure. Besides, though Mara hated herself for thinking it, a tiny but obstinate part of her was still reserving judgment on Adam himself. Though she saw no more than a generous, caring man and concerned father, she'd seen no warning signs from her fiancé, either.

When Adam thanked her for the compliment, his smile struck at the heart of her, struck her with the confidence that this man was no Jerry. She would stake her life on it.

And maybe she was.

Approaching the huge two-story house along a winding drive, she noticed that the ornate but tasteful wrought iron that ringed the house gave way to a transparent fence perhaps a hundred yards behind the back of the house, which faced the bluff's edge. While it made sense that Adam wouldn't block his gorgeous view of the surrounding rock formations and the town so far below, she wondered how sad he must feel, looking out each day over the very spot where his wife had fallen to her death.

As they pulled in to the garage, her phone rang. Pulling it from her bag, she sighed and looked at Adam. "It's Mrs. Rhodes."

"Go ahead and take it. I'll be right inside," he said, climbing from the car.

"I hope you're feeling better." Mrs. Rhodes sounded amazingly sincere for a woman who'd been threatening to fire her. "I've been so concerned."

"Thanks. I'm doing better," Mara said stiffly. "Well enough to return to school if—"

"About that, Mara." Mrs. Rhodes cleared her throat. "I've been talking about your, ah, situation with the superintendent. And we both agree, paid administrative leave's the best choice for the moment."

Mara's jaw dropped. "But that's what districts do when a teacher is under investigation. I haven't broken any laws."

"No one's accusing you, but this is a special situation. It's clear some unbalanced individual wishes to harm you. What if he were to show up during school hours? We certainly can't risk a situation like the one in Indiana."

Mara knew she was referring to a tragedy two months earlier, when a teacher's estranged husband had barged into her class and shot her, then himself, traumatizing a room full of fourth graders. The incident had been extensively reported in the media, amid calls for increased security in schools.

"Until the criminal who tried to harm you is caught," Mrs. Rhodes said, "I'm afraid we absolutely can't allow your presence to jeopardize staff and student safety."

As sensible as Mrs. Rhodes' precaution sounded, Mara couldn't help suspecting the woman was using this situation as an excuse to get rid of a "problem teacher." Because heaven forbid the principal should risk exposure to any new ideas. But there was no talking Jillian Rhodes out of her decision, in part because Mara had no idea how to defend herself, much less a class of second graders, from a threat she didn't understand.

As the conversation wrapped up, the door into the garage opened and Rebecca peeked out, her thin arms full of kitten, and her eyes so full of need and hope that Mara felt her objections to Adam's offer crumble into dust.

Chapter 9

"**W**ish I had some solid information for you, Jakes," Ronnie Rayburn said the next day.

Standing there in the sheriff's office, Adam was beginning to wonder whether the sheriff spent his time doing anything but politicking—and seducing disaffected housewives. "That's the same garbage I heard after Christine died, every day for months. I suppose you're going to rule this one an accident, as well? You think Mara Stillwell *accidentally* ducted that exhaust into her own casita?"

Rayburn had the stones to smirk. "Not likely. Still can't believe she didn't see it when she ran out to start the thing."

Adam shrugged. "She was in a hurry because of the rain, she told me. She hardly looked at the generator, except to use the electric starter. You come up with any prints?"

"Other than hers, just from your guys, and they all check out. And no witnesses saw anything suspicious, not there, not at the school, and not around your construction site."

"What about the phone threat? Mara said you were going to try and trace it through her service provider."

Rayburn made a show of pushing back his leather chair and crossing his ankles on his desktop, an obvious attempt to impress upon Adam that he was the man in charge here, before shaking his blond head. "Blocked call turned out to be from one of those pay-as-you-go cell phones, purchased for cash from the Flagstaff Wal-Mart. Just far away enough to stay anonymous."

"Somebody figured you'd be looking."

The sheriff cursed TV criminal investigation shows for educating criminals in the name of entertainment, then said, "You've still got your usual cretins committing crimes, but the smart ones, the ones that care if they get caught and think it through first…" He shook his head in disgust.

"So what's your theory on this?"

"Well, I can't come up with any credible reason why anybody'd want to hurt Miss Stillwell. Maybe a couple of ladies aren't so excited about her new teaching methods, but that's not what I would call a solid motive for murder."

Adam nodded, though it grated to agree with Rayburn.

The sheriff's wide-set gaze turned thoughtful. "Was wondering about you, though, whether there's been another lady in your life of late. Maybe the territorial type who'd take exception to you paying Mara special attention."

"A woman? You think a woman could have—"

Another shrug. "Those red footprints in Miss Stillwell's classroom were on the small side."

"Like a teenager's, Mara told me."

"Or a woman's."

Adam shook his head. "Since my wife, there's been no other woman." *Not till Mara.* Certainly Barbara Fairmont was interested, but he'd given her so little encouragement, he could hardly picture her obsessing. Knowing her reputation, she would just move on to another victim and try him again after her next marriage failed.

"You sure there was no one at all? C'mon, Mr. Jakes," Rayburn said. "Rich, good-looking fellow in his prime— wasn't there a one-night stand or two? A little phone sex, or maybe just a flirtation that went too far? We all have our weak moments."

"You slimy son of a—" Adam struggled to rein in his contempt for the man hiding safely behind his desk, his badge and his gun. "Don't even think of lumping me in with the likes of you. I've been busy with my project. Tied up tending to my daughter. A daughter I'm raising alone, thanks to—"

Jerking his feet off the desk, the sheriff rose to his feet, a warning in his hazel eyes. "I don't believe I'd go there. Not unless you want to be the richest man who's ever seen the inside of my jail."

Adam stood glaring, thinking it always came back to the money, the fortune he'd cobbled out of nothing but sheer nerve, student loans and sweat. No matter how hard he'd worked for it or how humble his background, people either envied, sucked up to or hated him by virtue of what he had that they didn't.

Rayburn's expression softened. "I know you want to blame me," he said thoughtfully. "And to tell the truth, I've asked myself the same questions. Whether something I did or didn't do helped drive Christine to that bluff. But did you ever stop to wonder if maybe you're focusing on my part, holding on to anger at me, so you don't have to look at yourself?"

"Why don't you skip the psychology and just find whoever's out to hurt Mara?"

"I will find him," the sheriff promised. "'Cause I'm damned well going to prove to you I *can*."

"You do that, Rayburn," was the best Adam could manage on his way out of the office.

Because if he stayed in there one more minute, he was either going to end up shot or behind bars.

* * *

At a low table in the house's library, Mara prompted Rebecca on a word from a story about a bear family struggling to trick a bee out of her honey. Freed from the worry of stumbling in front of her peers, the little girl was willing to "risk" sounding out words when needed, and she answered Mara's comprehension questions like a trouper.

"Hey, I have an idea," Mara said. "Let's write a story about the bee, how she feels about these big, hairy monsters taking all her honey."

Grinning, Rebecca shook one small fist. "I'll sting you all, you honey-stealers!" Turning a pleading look toward Mara, she added, "But can't I just draw it? I don't want to write."

Mara noticed the wheedling tone and the calculation gleaming in the girl's blue eyes. On her home turf, she was testing Mara, trying to find out how much she could get away with.

"I'll tell you what," Mara countered. "We'll write the story first. Then, if you work hard and do a good job, we'll make it into a storybook, with a front and back cover, and some illustrations—pictures."

"You mean like in a *real* book?" Excitement crept into the girl's voice.

"I do. Which means we have to make the story the very best it can be."

They worked for some time after that, Rebecca impressing Mara with her sustained effort and imagination. But no sooner had the girl started drawing than she veered totally off course, her pale eyes glazing over as she moved from the furious queen bee in the foreground to a deadly serious subject….

A familiar scene, this time silhouetted in the moonlight: one figure clearly pushing the other from a ledge. To Mara, both looked identical, prompting a new idea. Did the child mean to express, perhaps unconsciously, that her mother had destroyed herself?

Or did Rebecca truly believe that another woman had committed the murder on the bluffs? Had the child actually witnessed her mother's violent death?

This time, however, Mara decided to break the spell instead of just observing. To interrupt Rebecca's waking nightmare to try to find out what she dreamed.

Mara touched the child's arm, but it wasn't till she held it still that Rebecca looked up, surprise written in her eyes.

"What is it you're seeing?" Mara asked her. "Who is it you're drawing?"

Trembling, Rebecca glanced down at the picture, seeing it as if for the first time, before bursting into loud sobs, sobs that refused to ease no matter how hard Mara tried to offer comfort.

Minutes later, Rebecca raced upstairs, her bedroom door slamming behind her.

Mrs. Somers appeared at that moment, her hands on hips, to scowl at Mara. "What on earth are you doing to that child?"

Mara ached to follow Rebecca, but the housekeeper's fierce expression assured her that she was going nowhere without an explanation.

"I only asked her to tell me about the picture she was drawing. She was supposed to be illustrating a story we'd been working on, but instead she—"

"Those drawings…" Mrs. Somers fretted with her strand of pearls. "That poor child."

"So you've seen them?"

A troubled expression pinched Mrs. Somers' regal features. "I have indeed, and I can tell you, if you don't want her to completely shut down again, don't bother her about them. I won't have Rebecca upset like this. I can't bear to see her hurt any more."

"Do you really think I'm *trying* to upset her? Haven't I been working with her for months on my own time to get her talking?" From the first moment Mara had arrived here, she'd sensed Mrs. Somers' disapproval, but she couldn't let it go unchallenged. If the two of them didn't iron things out, Adam's longtime housekeeper, who had been with the family since Rebecca's second birthday, could make her own situation miserable.

"You've been working on *something,* all right. An M.R.S. degree to top off that bachelor's, from what I've heard."

"Who told you that?" Mara demanded.

Mrs. Somers stiffened, lifting her chin. "I have a friend who works for the mother of another of your students. And you'll never imagine what she overheard—what her Mrs. Fairmont saw with her own eyes going on between her son's teacher and my poor Mr. Jakes."

Red Bluff, Mara decided, ought to just change its name to Peyton Place and be done with it. "I'm here to teach Rebecca," she insisted.

With a disdainful sniff, the older woman brushed past her to stride toward the staircase calling, "Rebecca, please come out and have a cookie. Come sit with me and forget whatever your teacher did to make you cry."

Chapter 10

Just shy of midnight Friday, Adam answered the phone in his study, where he'd been listening to music and worrying over Rebecca's psychiatrist's recent advice on how to help her.

"Hi, Adam, this is Barbara." Whispering like a serpent through tall grasses, her voice raised the fine hairs on the back of his neck.

Revulsion quickly followed. "I'm surprised to hear from you, after our last conversation."

"I've been feeling bad about that." Her shift to poutiness came through loud and clear. "I don't want you being all mad at me."

"Then you should apologize to Mara Stillwell."

"I could do that, maybe. But first, I'd like the chance to make it up to you. I really *was* a very bad girl. When I saw the two of you together, my little green-eyed monster popped right out."

"Have you been drinking, Barbara?"

She giggled, a sound like fingernails raking down a

chalkboard. "Maybe a teensy bit. But mostly, I'm just lonely, Adam. Bored and lonely, and hoping for a little company to get me through it. Some strapping male company to see me through the night."

"I don't think so." He let his tone convey the "not in a million years" part.

But whether she was drunk, stubborn or flat-out crazy, Barbara kept on going, her voice going kittenish as she began describing the negligee that she was wearing, how she was taking it off and reaching down to touch—

Wincing, he said, "'Night, Barbara," and broke the connection. How the devil was he going to get it through that woman's head that he had no interest in her? Never had and never would, regardless of what he felt for Mara.

But it occurred to him that, hopeless though it was, Barbara wasn't giving up her bizarre fixation anytime soon. And that, despite his earlier skepticism, she might well have taken extreme steps to ensure she had no competition.

He wondered how extreme those steps might have been. Could she really have been responsible for the attempt on Mara's life? Or was it possible this went back all the way to Christine? He thought about his daughter's drawings, about the monstrous clawed hands she sometimes included in them.

No, that couldn't be it. *Couldn't.* It was insane to even think it. But by their very nature, obsessions weren't sane, and Barbara Fairmont was giving every sign that she'd slipped into obsession territory.

Still, he could all too easily imagine Ronnie Rayburn laughing off the idea that a woman of Barbara's reputation posed a danger because she'd called him seeking sex. Before Adam was willing to make a fool of himself with such a wild accusation, he was going to confront Barbara face-to-face.

Tomorrow, he decided, not wanting to take the slightest chance of seeing her with—or especially without—that negligee.

* * *

Alone since Rebecca had begged to take Jasper for the night, Mara lay back on the sumptuous burgundy bedding in her beautifully appointed guest suite, a set of rooms more spacious than any place she'd ever lived as an adult. She could have pushed a button to automatically screen the huge window so she would be able to sleep in the following morning. Instead, she stayed awake, watching for the meteors that occasionally streaked across the star field, as she tried—and failed—to put Barbara Fairmont's ugly gossip out of her mind.

The woman was like a cracked barrel of toxic waste in the town reservoir, poisoning minds against her, from Jillian Rhodes to the other PTO mothers all the way to Mrs. Somers, who was undermining Mara's efforts to help Rebecca and darting suspicious looks across the table where Adam insisted they all take meals together.

How long would it be before Babzilla managed to taint Mara's relationship with Adam, too? She fell asleep wondering what she could possibly do, short of leaving town, to solve the problem.

Sometime later, the soft trill of her cell phone woke her. Half-asleep, she reached for it, murmuring, "Hello?"

A grotesque voice warped the night around her. *"Her nails were torn, did you know? Ripped from where she clung to the bluff's edge—until he stomped down on her fingers. Are you hanging on tight, little teacher? Waiting for the other shoe to drop?"*

"Barbara Fairmont," Mara managed, though she couldn't be sure. But there was something feminine, she thought, in the cadence of the artificially distorted words, the tenor of the phrasing. "I swear, I'm going to call the sheriff. This is sick. Just crazy."

Laughter followed—definitely female. *"You're as stupid as you are stubborn, little teacher. So be it. You've been warned."*

Hot fury had Mara shooting back, "This time, try coming after me to my face and see what it gets you, you psycho." But she was yelling at dead air, she realized. The caller's way of getting the last word.

And then she jumped at a tapping at her door. A knock that froze the blood in her veins. Had her tormenter, the very person who'd already tried once to kill her, been calling from *inside* the house?

"Mara?" called a muffled voice. "Mara, are you all right?"

Relief rushed through her, and she cried, "Adam!"

The door opened, and she saw him, a large figure lit only by the skim-milk moonlight. "What's wrong? I was passing by, and I heard—"

"She called again and threatened me. She said —"

"Oh, Mara." Closing the door behind him, he came to her, sitting on the bed's edge and pulling her into his arms.

She melted into him, her entire body shaking, grateful for the comfort that could only be communicated by a human touch. *His* touch.

"So Rayburn was right?" he asked quietly. "It really is a woman?"

Mara nodded. "The voice was disguised again, but there was something about it that made me think so."

"Tell me, what did she say?" His big hands smoothed her hair down her back. "All of it, while it's still fresh in your mind."

She hesitated, hating herself for the ribbon of doubt that snaked along her backbone. Not long ago, she'd watched a news special about a man believed responsible for the death or disappearance of three wives. Charming and successful, he'd never had the slightest difficulty in attracting a new lover, in spite of the highly publicized suspicion.

Could she be one of those foolish women? A woman who trusted her heart to a killer?

"Please, Mara," he urged, settling a soft kiss against her temple.

A kiss that melted away her hesitation. This was *Adam*, a man whose gentleness belied his power, a man she knew instinctively would fight to the death to protect even the most flawed wife. A man who, rather than accepting the easy out of a ruling of accidental death, had earned the sheriff's enmity by hiring private detectives to investigate the matter.

A man who had been just outside her door at two in the morning.

"It's the middle of the night," she said. "What were you doing? 'Just passing by' my room?" His bedroom was upstairs with the others, a territory she pointedly avoided, though she'd spent too many restless hours contemplating the second floor since she had moved in. And particularly what lay behind his door.

"When I can't sleep, I pace."

"You haven't slept well lately." She'd noticed the smudges of exhaustion beneath his eyes, had heard Mrs. Somers say over meals that he'd been working too hard. "I know you're worried about Rebecca, worried about whether to put her on medication."

Adam squeezed Mara even harder. "That's not the only thing that's made me restless," came his whispered admission. "Not the only reason I find myself walking past your door and thinking about…about keeping you safe."

"I'm here," she answered, her mouth so close to his that she could feel the warmth of his breath, making her lips tingle. "Safe in your house." *Safe in your arms…*

"You *are* keeping me up nights," he confessed. "Knowing you're so damned close, but that I can't—I gave my word I'd never—"

Resolve shattering, Mara kissed him, needing to feel his mouth against hers, to taste the desire that flowed like electricity between them.

A groan of raw hunger rose from his throat as he pressed her back into the pillows. The kiss caught fire, an urgent conflagration that had her melting like a candle. She couldn't keep her hands off him, couldn't stop herself from fumbling with the buttons of his shirt.

Stripping back the top sheet, Adam mouthed his way to her breasts, suckling her right through the silky fabric of her nightgown. Pleasure arced straight through her, bowing her back with a need so powerful it obliterated every other concern.

In a frenzy of desire, they undressed each other, and she drew another moan from him as she laid her hands on the hard, hot length of him and lightly bit his neck.

"Yes," she told him, "please, yes," as his fingers found and stroked the damp center of her, as blue-hot sparks skated around the edges of her vision.

"Now," she urged. "Please, Adam."

He moved over her, his knees between her thighs, his words shaking with a hard-won vestige of control. "Say it again, Mara. Say my name again. Now."

She looked up into his face, all moonlight and dark shadow. "I want you, Adam. I need to feel all of you. *Now…*"

After an almost-unbearable delay, she moaned in relief as he pushed deep inside her. Rocking her body while he took her, whispering into her ear, "Want you. I want you so much, Mara," as the two of them settled into a rhythm as ancient as the moon outside the window.

And as sure and right and perfect as the starlight in her eyes.

Chapter 11

"**W**hat if your daughter needed you? Did you ever stop to think of that?" Dressed in a quilted floral robe with her gray-streaked hair worn loose, Mrs. Somers stared at Adam over her favorite teacup, her disapproval barely softened by the rosy light of dawn. She must have heard the door to Mara's room close and then crept out to catch him in the hallway.

Ordinarily, he wouldn't tolerate being confronted like a teenager in his own home, but his concern for his daughter trumped his irritation. "Did Rebecca wake you up? She didn't have another bad dream, did she?"

"No, but let's suppose she had and couldn't find you. Or, worse yet, found you with that woman. It would be quite a shock. Not to mention, if you don't mind me saying so, extremely inappropriate to expose a young child to such goings on, especially with her teacher."

"I *do* mind you saying so," he said firmly, but the rare glimmer of moisture in her eyes gave him pause, as did the memory of this past year's quiet conversations over morning tea, when they'd sat together talking about Rebecca or the details of the household, but never about the spouses they'd lost, not her husband years before or Adam's wife so much more recently.

He owed her for her steadfast loyalty, her stolid Yankee sensibility, and her concern. Owed her more than to treat her like an hourly employee.

"You know what? You make a good point about my daughter," he admitted. "One I'll carefully consider. But I won't be made to feel guilty, and I won't lie and say I'm going to stay away from Mara. Neither of us intended for this to happen, but I care for her very much."

"Are you certain of that?" Mrs. Somers pressed. "That *she* didn't *intend* this from the moment she chose to move to Red Bluff?"

Adam frowned at her. "You've always said you didn't hold with gossip."

Her cheeks flushed as if she had been slapped. "That may be true, but I can't stick my head in the sand, either, not when it comes to the members of this family. And certainly not when a simple computer search of her name leads me to an article about a certain thief arrested in New Jersey, a thief who happens to have been engaged to—"

"That's enough. How would you like Mara trying to dig up dirt on you?" Noticing Mrs. Somers' wounded look, Adam touched her bony hand. "I understand you're only looking out for us. But I know all about Mara's ex-fiancé, and he doesn't matter. What matters is that she makes me very happy—and she makes my daughter happy, too."

"Except when she has her in tears," Mrs. Somers murmured.

But when Adam responded with a sharp look, she abruptly rose from her seat, and said it was high time she went to run her weekly errands.

* * *

Mara went into the kitchen to find Adam standing at the window, staring at the sun-washed landscape, and found herself eager to feel his arms around her once more.

He looked at her with sad eyes, taking in her jeans and soft green sweater, though a smile wavered on his lips.

"Everything all right?" She stopped short, struck suddenly with doubt. Was he regretting making love with her?

"Just preoccupied," he admitted, closing the gap between them and taking her hand, using his callused thumb to stroke flesh still soft from her shower.

"About the phone call?" she asked. "Or something else?"

She stopped there, unable to hold on to a thought as he drew her hand toward his mouth. When he kissed her fingers, pleasure rippled through her, an echo of those lips caressing other places.

Too soon, he released her, unease flickering in his dark eyes. "I'm wondering if it's possible I took advantage last night. You were upset, trying to tell me about that phone call, and you *are* living under my roof."

"What happened between us, it's been building these past few months. And since that kiss at the school…" Groping for words, she shook her head. "I've been feeling a little like a lit fuse, no matter how hard I've fought against it."

"Yes, that's it exactly. You can't imagine how many nights I've lain awake thinking about you." But instead of pulling her close, he dropped her hand and kept his distance. "But we do need to be careful. There's Rebecca, of course, and unfortunately, Mrs. Somers caught me coming out of your room. I'm sorry if that's going to make things uncomfortable between you. I've spoken with her, of course, but—"

"I doubt you'll change her mind. Mrs. Somers has already had her head filled with all kinds of rumors about my 'gold-digging ways.'" Mara's fingers hooked tiny quotes in the air.

"Has she been rude to you? Made you feel unwelcome?"

Mara shook her head. "Don't blame her, please. She's only trying to protect you and Rebecca."

He gave a derisive snort. "I blame Barbara Fairmont for spreading rumors all over town. And that's not all. Not long before you received that anonymous call last night, she phoned me. Invited me to come and see her. Sounded pretty smashed."

Mara gave a mock shudder. "A drunken booty call from Babzilla—now *there's* a scary thought."

Adam's smile was short-lived. "It gets a whole lot scarier if she was the one who called you afterward."

Sobering instantly, Mara wound her arms around herself for warmth. "Whoever called me sounded stone-cold sober." Those words had been too cruel, too calculating, to have come from someone who was wasted.

"Tell me what she said." The suggestion of a smile played in his dark eyes. "And this time, I'll try not to sidetrack you."

She hesitated, flustered by thoughts of the way he'd distracted her last night. Turning to hide her blush, she asked, "Would you like some coffee?"

"I've had some, but the rest of the pot should still be fresh."

She poured herself a cup as she haltingly, reluctantly, recounted the entire conversation. Including the hideous suggestion that he had killed his wife.

"I'm sorry," she finished, the words lying bitter in her mouth. "I didn't want to have to tell you that part."

Afterward, there was a long silence, which she broke by suggesting, "The sheriff needs to know about this call, too. No matter what you think of him, he should talk to Barbara—"

Glancing at Adam, she froze at the sight of the man who had loved her so tenderly only hours before. He looked up at her, trembling with anger, his jaw clenched tight and his dark eyes ablaze with fury.

"I need to smash something." The quiet control in his voice frightened her more than the loudest raving would have. "Or drive down to that woman's house and shake that empty blond head right off her shoulders."

"They're only lies, that's all," Mara whispered, turning toward him. "Cruel lies from a coward, meant to hurt you." She reached out but couldn't quite bring herself to touch him, instinct screaming a shrill warning that he might at any moment erupt into violence.

He stared at her hand before looking up into her eyes, his expression devastated. "You *believe* it, don't you?" he demanded. "You're asking yourself this morning 'Did I make a terrible mistake? Make love with a man who murdered his own wife? A man who crushed her fingers to make her let go of—'"

She jerked her hand away. "*No,* of course I don't believe it. Are you crazy? Whoever this lunatic is, she's already tried to kill me. Why on earth would I believe *her?*"

Yet in spite of Mara's denial, the caller's words rang through her mind. *Are you hanging on tight, little teacher? Waiting for the other shoe to drop?*

Worse yet was the question that echoed through her heart. Was it remotely possible she'd placed her trust in the wrong man? Just as she had with Jerry not so long ago?

Adam saw her doubt, seized on it. "If you don't believe what she said, then why won't you touch me? Why *can't* you?"

Hard as it was, she met his gaze and held it. "You're angry, and you're hurting. But that gives you absolutely no right to take it out on me. Especially not after last night."

"No, Daddy!" cried a small voice. "No more fighting."

Turning, Mara saw Rebecca, still wearing pajamas, her hair mussed with sleep and her face wet with tears.

"Please, Daddy. Don't make her die, too."

Chapter 12

Heart jackhammering against his chest wall, Adam fell to his knees beside his daughter, his instinct prompting him to drag the crying child into his arms. "Shh, everything's all right, I promise."

He stroked her hair, then used a clean dish towel that a moon-pale Mara passed him to blot Rebecca's tears. When her sobs abated somewhat, he asked, "What do you mean, honey? Are you talking about your mama?"

Clamming up, she wouldn't make eye contact, not even when he tilted her chin, forcing her to face him.

"Please, Rebecca," he pleaded. *"Please, just tell us. No one will be mad."*

Mara squatted down beside him and cupped the girl's cheek. "I'm right here. I'm not going anywhere."

Rebecca looked up, her pale eyes gleaming.

"I'm safe," Mara persisted. "You're safe. Your daddy's safe, too. But we need you to tell us, are you scared because of what happened to your mother?"

After a long pause, the child nodded.

"Are you…?" Adam faltered, sickened by the idea that his daughter—his beating heart—might fear him. Steeling himself, he forced out the question, "Are you afraid I hurt her? Is that what you think?"

Quivering violently, Rebecca shook her head. Did that mean she believed in him, he wondered, or was she terrified he would hurt her, too? Emotion searing his eyes, Adam felt his throat cinch tight.

Mara knelt beside Rebecca. "Everybody has little disagreements sometimes. Why would you think something like that might hurt me?"

When the girl didn't answer, Mara asked, "Does this have anything to do with the pictures you've been drawing? The pictures of the lady falling?"

Again there was no answer, so Adam asked her, "Are you afraid that if we argue, Miss Stillwell might hurt herself? Is that what you think happened with your mama?" Had his daughter heard him arguing with Christine about the affair she had admitted to? Or had she overheard him later, begging his wife to keep her counseling appointments?

Or did you leave our child a legacy of mental illness, Christine? Cold waves rippled over him, the fevered chill of raw fear.

Rebecca stared blankly ahead, her blue eyes glazed over, and nothing that either he or Mara did drew a response.

Looking from his immobile child to Mara, he asked, "What now? What should I do?"

"Do you have an emergency contact number for one of the counselors you've worked with? Someone Rebecca trusts?"

Adam had never felt so helpless. Shaking his head, he said miserably, "My daughter trusts *you,* Mara."

She grasped his hand and squeezed it, shaking her head. "This is way beyond me, Adam. Call the child psychiatrist. Call right now and ask what we should do."

* * *

All three of them made the hour-long drive to Flagstaff, where Dr. Millstadt met them, concerned enough by what he'd heard to come to the office on a Saturday.

After examining Rebecca, who had come around enough to take an interest in the paper and crayons in his office, the bespectacled, slump-shouldered man in a cardigan sweater waved Adam toward him.

"Come on, Mara," Adam invited. "You're a part of this, too."

She nodded, moved by the heartbreak in his eyes. As she stood by his side, shame seeped to the surface, a deep flush prompted by the memory of her own doubts.

When Dr. Millstadt gestured toward a grouping of chairs, they all sat, both Mara and Adam positioning themselves where they could watch Rebecca.

Focusing mainly on Adam, the doctor spoke calmly, his deep voice conveying professional concern. "I know you've been resisting the medication option, but your daughter shows signs of an acute anxiety disorder, probably brought on by last year's trauma." He passed Adam a prescription. "This can help her relax enough to talk out her issues in counseling, which is something I highly recommend. Other than some initial drowsiness as her body adapts to the dosage, side effects are rare and mild. I think you should consider it, for your daughter's sake."

Adam frowned down at the slip of paper. "I should be able to reach my own child without resorting to pills. I should... I'm her father. I should be able to fix this."

Beside him, Mara touched his elbow, hurting for him as much as for Rebecca.

Behind his wire-rimmed glasses, the doctor's magnified, brown eyes were sympathetic. "I understand your frustration, Mr. Jakes, and I've seen how hard you've been working to help Rebecca. But this isn't about you now. It's about easing your daughter's suffering long enough to let her heal."

When Adam hesitated, Mara laid her hand on his wrist. "Please, let's try this, Adam, for Rebecca's sake. At least give the medicine a chance."

He swallowed audibly, his gaze never leaving his daughter. Glancing the child's way, Mara saw, even from across the room, that she was busy coloring another falling picture.

In this one, Rebecca's mother's face was bloody, and her hair had turned the same deep auburn shade as Mara's own.

By the time he finally got his daughter tucked in for the night, Adam was exhausted from the stress of worrying and angry with himself for giving in to other people's prodding. And guilty as hell after watching Rebecca slide into a drugged stupor that reminded him painfully of the aftermath of Christine's worst episodes. Was his child, the only family he had left, slipping away from him, as well? Would this medication prove a help, or would it be the first curve of the downward spiral that, one way or another, had eventually consumed her mother?

Mrs. Somers caught him just outside his daughter's bedroom. Though the light spilling down the hall was dim, he saw that her spine was stiff and her cheeks splashed with color, as if she were gearing up for battle. "I can't stand seeing her this way. Those doctors and their pills couldn't save Christine, and they won't save—"

"Don't. You. Start. With me," he warned, before stalking past her.

At the bottom of the stairs, he found Mara waiting for him, alarm tightening her features, either because of what she had heard or what she saw now in his eyes. As she opened her mouth to speak, he snapped, "I don't want to be placated right now. Don't want to hear one more word on how I'm doing the right thing."

From upstairs came the sound of Mrs. Somers' quiet snuffling before a bedroom door snapped shut.

"You want to be upset," Mara told him, "that's fine. If you need to take it out on *the help,* we'll get over it. But suck it up and focus on your daughter, Adam. Rebecca's carrying a secret, and if this medication can help unlock it, she'll move on. She'll heal. I know she will."

"I said I don't want to hear this."

Mara's green eyes flamed. "If you think your guest suite and a paycheck buy you the right to shut me up, forget it. I'm here because I love Rebecca. Because I want the best for her."

"You're here because you have nowhere else to go," he shot back, regretting his temper even as the cruel words exploded from him.

As she spun away from him, he said, "I didn't mean that, Mara. It's been a really long— I'm being an idiot. I know that."

She glared over her shoulder. "When you're ready to be a human being again, we're going to get some things straight. But you're right about one thing. It's been a long day, and I'm going to bed. And by the way, the door to my room will be locked, so don't even think about trying to slip inside, *boss.*"

"Mara," he called as she stalked away from him. "I'm sorry. I don't think of you as some employee. And I don't know what I'd do without—"

When she stopped, she didn't turn to face him, but her voice betrayed her tears. "Tomorrow. We can talk tomorrow, Adam. But no more tonight. No more."

Defeated for the moment, he let her walk away from him.

Chapter 13

Adam holed up in his home office in a bid to distract himself with work, but while business kept him busy, it barely smoothed the surface of his worry.

Distracted, he didn't notice the flashing light on his answering machine until he was nearly finished. Frowning, he pressed the play button.

"Adam, this is Barbara." The silken seductiveness of her voice turned Adam's stomach. *"I'm afraid I might have said something to offend you last night. I'm known to do that after one too many glasses of the bubbly...."*

The squeak of her giggle nearly drove him to hang up, but her recorded voice soon sobered. *"If you stop by tonight, I'm almost certain I can make it up to you. And I'm absolutely positive you'll like the way I apologize."*

Sickened, he wondered if it was truly possible that the woman had lost her mind, plunging over the edge that separated a cunning mantrap from a stalker. But one thing was certain. Sheriff Rayburn would laugh him out of the office if he came in with nothing but this tape and a theory based on nothing but speculation and Mara's belief that her caller had been female.

As Adam considered, he noticed for the first time that the wind had picked up outside, as it often did atop the bluffs. As well insulated as the windows were, he heard the air's cold rush, the hiss of sand against the glass that sounded like a bad recording.

It gave him an idea, a way to get the solid proof he needed to take to Rayburn. Digging through a desk drawer, Adam found a pocket digital recorder he hadn't used in several years. After replacing its batteries and testing it, he went to Mrs. Somers' room, where he apologized for his rude response to her earlier concern…

…and then he told her he was leaving and might be gone for hours.

Mara had no idea how long she'd been sleeping when the pounding started: a heavy, rapid knocking that jerked her suddenly awake.

"The house had better be on fire, Adam," she grumbled as she climbed out of bed and shuffled to the door, not caring that she'd opted for the comfort of old flannel pajama bottoms and an even older college sweatshirt. Served him right for first insulting her, then scaring her half to death.

But instead of Adam, it was Mrs. Somers, still dressed for the day, with her eyes wide, and her face as white and fragile as bone china. "Rebecca's gone. She's not in her room. I looked everywhere, and then I found the back door standing open."

Oh, God. What if she'd been taken? Taken by whoever had been behind the calls, the vandalism at the school and the resort site, and the attack on her own life? A recent news report flashed through her brain, the story of an unhinged mother who'd used the internet to stalk her nine-year-old's class rival. Could Barbara Fairmont be insane enough to go even further?

No. It couldn't be true. Maybe Rebecca had been sleepwalking and now lay curled up in a corner somewhere. Could the new medication be to blame?

"Where's Adam?" Mara asked frantically. "Is he looking for her?"

"He's not at home!" the older woman cried. "And when I called his cell phone, I only got his voice mail."

Before Mara could process what she'd said, Mrs. Somers added, "Hurry, please. We have to find her."

Mara shoved her bare feet into slippers and ran after Mrs. Somers. Before she'd gone three steps, she felt a cold draft from the open back door. Desperately, she asked, "Are you sure she's not here somewhere?"

"I'd stake my life on it," Mrs. Somers called over her shoulder as she headed for a closet just off the kitchen. "When I went to check on her, I found the kitten shut in her room but no Rebecca anywhere. Please, we need to hurry, before it's too late."

Opening the closet, the housekeeper frantically pawed through the hangers. "Her coat's still in here. If she's gone out into this cold without one…"

As Mrs. Somers grabbed her own coat, Mara asked, "You know where she is, don't you?"

And then Mara realized that she knew, too, prompted by her own instinct, coupled with picture after picture that the girl had drawn. "She's gone to the bluff, hasn't she? To where her mother fell."

"Don't leave. Please don't go," Barbara Fairmont begged him as she stood in the driveway of her custom golf course home. She should have been freezing, wearing no more than a whisper-thin white peignoir over the bare suggestion of a negligee, but thanks to the champagne flute in her hand, Adam doubted she felt anything except a crashing sense of doom.

Tipsy as she was, she'd allowed him to get a glimpse of the papers lying on a writing table in her study. Forms announcing the impending foreclosure on her house, which explained her desperation to quickly find a man to "save" her. And who better than the newly single owner of the largest bank account in town?

But no matter how financially needy and terminally horny she might be, Barbara was no killer. Angry, yes, she proved as she hurled her champagne at his retreating Jaguar, but in the long run, more pitiful than dangerous.

Adam pulled out his cell phone at a stop sign and reluctantly called the sheriff's office. He was surprised to be put straight through to Rayburn himself.

"This is Adam Jakes," he said by way of greeting. "You're working late tonight."

"What can I do for you?" Rayburn asked curtly. "Any more vandalism at your worksite?"

"No, it's Barbara Fairmont. I think you ought to do a welfare check. It's a cold night, she's been drinking, and last I saw her, she was standing outside her house in next to nothing." That ought to get Rayburn's attention. "I'd take it as a personal favor if you'd stop by and make sure she's all right."

"A personal favor? You and she aren't—I thought you were shacked up with that teacher?"

Much as he hated Rayburn, Adam would not be baited. "I'm not involved with Barbara, but I had reason to suspect she might've been the one threatening Mara, who got another call last night."

Rayburn gave a derisive snort. "I can tell you, Barbara's one woman who doesn't have to resort to threats and murder attempts to attract a man's attention." The admiring rumble of Rayburn's voice assured Adam that the sheriff had spent some time in her bed.

Could the two of them have been spending time there recently? Adam felt a sick chill snake around his gut. Maybe Barbara didn't have it in her to commit the acts that Adam had suspected, but what if she'd been coached and prompted? Manipulated by a man eager to pay Adam back for endangering his job? Could someone else be in on the plot with them—if such a plot existed?

"Just check on Barbara—if you really give a damn about her," Adam told him before breaking the connection.

At the moment he wanted nothing more than to get home and make things right with Mara—if she hadn't decided he was really a killer after all.

Chapter 14

Horror exploded inside Mara, cold terror as she imagined Rebecca slipping through some unguessed gap in the fence to stand alone out on the bluff. "Have you called the sheriff?"

Mrs. Somers pulled two flashlights from a shelf. "They'd take too long to get here. Please hurry. I have my phone. I'll call someone on the way."

Mara reached into the closet and grabbed the first coat she reached, a long red wool one. It was far longer than her own, and from the way Mrs. Somers gaped at her, eyes glassy, Mara surmised it had once belonged to Christine.

"Let's go," Mara urged, grabbing one of the flashlights and heading out into the wind-scoured night. A frigid gust induced instant chill bumps.

She tried to look past the older woman, who was still standing in the doorway. Mara thought she had heard something, a sound from inside, barely audible above the wind. "What was that?" she asked. But Mrs. Somers didn't budge.

"Daddy?" Rebecca's faint voice floated toward her. From the staircase, Mara thought, relief surging hot through her veins.

Hadn't Mrs. Somers heard the child?

"That's Rebecca calling." Mara felt a grin forming. "From inside—upstairs."

As she still stood there like a statue, Mrs. Somers' face went stone still. Certain the other woman was in shock, Mara attempted to push past her and return to the house.

And stopped dead when she saw the gun in the housekeeper's hand, the short barrel pointed straight at Mara's chest.

Shock slammed her, dropping her stomach to her knees. "What are you doing? Put that away—now."

"I don't take orders from the likes of you."

Seeing the fierce determination in Mrs. Somers' face, Mara said, "Please, Rebecca needs you. She's calling for you right now."

"Don't. You. Move." Taking one step backward, Mrs. Somers turned her head slightly—still watching Mara carefully—and raised her voice to call, "Rebecca, dear. Go back to bed now. Your daddy will be home soon to tuck you in."

"I want Miss Stillwell," the girl answered.

"You will go to your room now," Mrs. Somers said harshly. "Unless you want that wretched kitten sleeping outdoors in the cold where it belongs."

Rebecca began crying.

"He's going out on the bluff, Rebecca," Mrs. Somers told her, "if you don't get straight back to bed this instant."

Moments later, they heard the distant sound of a door slamming.

"You *bitch*." Mara took a step closer. "You heartless— She knows, doesn't she? That's what's wrong with Rebecca. She knows it was *you* who killed her mother. Was she there that night? Did that poor child see you do it?"

Backlit by the inside light, Mrs. Somers stiffened. "It was all for her, for her and Mr. Jakes. That woman wasn't fit to be a mother to that girl, and she certainly didn't deserve a fine man like my Adam. Cheating on him, she was, then wailing and whining around about the guilt it cost her. Cost *her,* as if she weren't some filthy harlot."

"And you think being a murderer is better? Don't you see how you're hurting Rebecca, destroying the same child you meant to save?"

"Everything was fine with my family." The housekeeper's storm-gray eyes were anguished. "With Rebecca and her father. The three of us were happy—very, very happy—before *you* came along."

Praying that she was guessing correctly, that the child was the key, Mara said, "Rebecca barely spoke. She wasn't functioning on any level. Is that what you call happy?"

Mrs. Somers lashed out, cracking the revolver against Mara's forehead. Crying out with pain, Mara tried to jump back, but her legs folded, dropping her onto her hands and knees.

"How dare you?" Mrs. Somers railed. "I've cared for that child since she was only two. She was always far more mine than Christine's."

Wiping blood from her forehead, Mara used the door frame to pull herself to her feet. Above her, the night sky spun, the horizon tilting and the full moon flashing bright. "I only meant to help her. Surely you want her to get better. You must want what's best for—"

"I warned you and warned you to leave town. I did everything but kill you, and what did you do but come to *my* home and flaunt your body in front of Adam until he could see nothing else."

"Please, Rebecca needs us—all of us—working to help her," Mara implored. Sick and dangerous as her obsession was, Mrs. Somers clearly cared for the girl.

"I won't have her loving you!" Mrs. Somers shouted, eyes burning with jealousy. "And I won't have him ever touching you again. Now move. We're going for a walk, girl."

Mara glanced around, looking for anywhere to flee, any way to fight.

"Try it and I *will* shoot," Mrs. Somers warned her. "I'd rather go to prison than allow the likes of you to take my family from me, to be the one to raise *my* child."

Mara's mouth went chalk dry. There was no reasoning with insanity—and no running from a bullet, either. But maybe she could overpower the older woman—if she remained alive long enough to find an opportunity. And horrible as the thought was, if it came down to her own death, Mara didn't want it happening where Rebecca might bear witness.

"Drop the flashlight and raise your hands where I can see them," Mrs. Somers ordered. "And walk. Walk out the gate and toward the edge."

Adam had expected to come home to a dark house. Instead, he found lights on and the place as cold as a tomb. He ran through the downstairs to the back door and found a bright red smear staining the open doorway—a streak that looked like fresh blood.

Dear God. Had an intruder somehow bypassed the security to break in, then killed or injured—

"Rebecca!" Heart in his throat, he raced up the stairs, flipping on more lights. "Mara! Mrs. Somers!"

His daughter burst out of her bedroom and flung herself into his shaking arms. "You have to help her, Daddy. You have to save her this time," she said before disintegrating into sobs.

"Save who? *Who,* Rebecca?"

Weeping too hard for coherent speech, she pointed downstairs, in the direction of Mara's room. Scooping Rebecca into his arms, Adam paused, then rushed back to

Mrs. Somers' room, which he found empty, before pounding down the steps.

"Where did they go?" he asked his daughter, who was clinging to his neck so tightly he felt as if he were choking. "You have to tell me. Who took them?"

Hurrying to Mara's bedroom, he threw open the door and called her name. No answer.

"No, Daddy. No," Rebecca finally managed, and he saw her pointing toward the open back door.

Toward the door and the bluff's edge beyond it, where he couldn't bear to imagine what horror he might find.

Chapter 15

With Rebecca in his arms, Adam called 9-1-1, then found a flashlight in the garage, along with a small utility knife, which he tucked inside his jacket.

"I need you to stay here," he told his daughter, but she clung even tighter, weeping so piteously that he raced outside with her, running toward the bluff.

Had it been Mara's blood, smeared inside the door frame? After all, she had already been the target of one attempt on her life. Had the threats and the destruction been about her all along?

From the rocks ahead, he heard a female voice, whipped by freezing wind and strong emotion. He couldn't make out the words, but he thought it might be Mara, arguing with someone.

Instinct brought her name almost to his lips, but then he realized surprise might be his best weapon, his only hope of saving the two women from whoever had abducted them.

Because he couldn't just sit around and wait for Rayburn

and his deputies to get there. He had already failed Christine; he wasn't about to risk Mara's life, or Mrs. Somers', either.

Setting Rebecca down, he hugged the shivering child against him and realized he'd failed her, too, carrying her so close to danger. "I need you to go back to our house. Once you get there, lock yourself inside my office and dial 9-1-1. Tell them where you are, and where I'm going."

Digging her short nails into his hand, Rebecca looked up, terror in her moonlit face and pale eyes. "You have to save her this time. You can't let Mrs.—Mrs.—" She struggled to get the words out, failed.

But Adam understood—Rebecca was terrified that something would happen to the housekeeper who had taken care of her for as long as she could remember. "Don't be scared, please, sweetheart. Now be a big girl for me and go back inside where it's warm."

After watching her start toward the house, he heard a shriek. Forgetting everything else, he rushed toward the spot, his flashlight beam ranging ahead…

…and touching on a violent struggle near the bluff's edge, not between Mara, Mrs. Somers and some unknown assailant—but between Mrs. Somers and…Christine. But how could his dead wife…?

Stunned, he froze, then realized it was Mara he saw—Mara wearing Christine's red coat as she struggled to grasp Mrs. Somers' right hand.

The hand that held a gun.

"No!" he roared, his voice reverberating off the star-washed rock as he instinctively pulled the knife from his pocket. "Drop it. Drop the weapon, Mrs. Somers. Now."

Startled by his shout, the housekeeper gaped in his direction. Taking advantage of the other woman's distraction, Mara twisted to snatch the revolver from Mrs. Somers' hand.

It should have ended there—and would have, except that

Mara's legs tangled in the long coat. Stumbling, she went down hard, rolling over the cliff's edge with a shrill, truncated scream.

Mara fell, her body twisting before she slammed down onto a narrow shelf. There was a loud snap, her left elbow cracking as it struck rock first, and the gun she had been holding spun over the side.

She nearly followed, her momentum carrying her close to the edge before her fingers clutched rock as one leg swung out over empty space. Pain exploded through her injured elbow, kaleidoscopic color bursting through her vision.

Yet she hung on, even as the strength drained from her left hand. Hung on and pulled herself back to safety, where she shuddered uncontrollably and listened to the shouting somewhere above.

"You killed her." Anguish poured through Adam's words, a grief so raw that Mara couldn't doubt his feelings for her. "You killed her, and you killed Christine, *didn't you?*"

"What? No!" shrieked the older woman. "Mara attacked *me*. Marched me here at gunpoint and said she'd get me out of her way so she can have you all to herself."

Galvanized by fury, Mara uncurled herself and looked up to the lip of rock perhaps six feet above. Looked up and then felt around to find a crack in the sheer rock face, a jutting stone at her hip level. Dangerous hand- and footholds, but there was no time to find better.

"Stop lying!" Adam shouted. "I saw the blood on her face, the gun in your hand. I know it was you. My God, no wonder Rebecca's been so—and now you've killed *Mara*, too?"

Hot tears coursed down Mara's face as she hauled herself still higher, too out of breath to speak, to tell him that she was alive.

"You have it all wrong," Mrs. Somers pleaded. "I wrestled

the gun from her. That's why I had it. I swear, *she* was trying to kill *me*."

"Why, Mrs. Somers—Dora? Why would you do this?"

One more step. That's all I need, thought Mara. With her left arm useless, she fought to push herself up with her legs.

"Don't you understand?" Mrs. Somers wailed. "*I'm* Rebecca's mother, just as truly as if she'd come out of my own womb. We could have been perfect, the three of us. The perfect family. We still can, if you'll just—"

"You're insane. Now get back from the—"

"It's all ruined anyway. She ruined everything. I see that."

"*Stop,*" Adam ordered. "Stay away from—"

Mara was close now, so close to their voices. Reaching her hand upward, she touched the edge…

…of a *shoe?* She barely moved her fingers in time to keep from being stepped on.

Bracing herself on bruised knees, she stared upward as an arm swung out over the edge. Was it Mrs. Somers? Did she mean to throw herself off the same bluff where she'd tried to push Mara?

"No," Mara said, recoiling instinctively for fear of being knocked back down, perhaps to topple all two hundred feet this time.

At the sound of her voice, Mrs. Somers shrieked in surprise, and there was a grunt as Adam tackled her and pressed her flat atop the bluff's edge. With his body pinning the struggling woman, he stretched his hand into the darkness, saying, "Mara? Mara, is that you?"

"Adam," Mara gasped back, clutching him with her right hand. Holding on and swearing she would never let him go.

Epilogue

"Be careful with her, baby," Adam told his daughter the next afternoon as they approached Mara, who was dressed and ready to leave the hospital where she'd spent the night. "You wouldn't want to squeeze her too tight and hurt that broken arm."

Mara had other bumps and bruises, as well, enough that the doctor hadn't objected when Adam insisted she be kept for observation.

"Are you kidding?" Mara asked, falling to her knees beside the bed to kiss and hug Rebecca. "Your hugs are exactly what the doctor ordered."

Smiling up at Adam, she added, "And so are *your* kisses."

"You've had plenty," he joked, though he doubted there could ever be enough kisses to reassure himself that she was whole and safe beside him, in spite of last night's horror. He still saw her falling every time he closed his eyes.

"The sheriff came," Rebecca reported, her expression

earnest. "And he told me they had *her* locked up tight, where she can never hurt me."

"They'll put Mrs. Somers in a special hospital," Adam reassured her, "where she won't be able to hurt *anyone* again."

"And she won't be allowed to come back to our house *ever*," the girl added, her relief filling Adam with the hope that, with love and patient understanding, she would survive the past year's trauma with her spirit intact.

When a knock came, Mara stood. "Finally, my discharge papers. Come in, please."

Instead of the nurse they had expected, Principal Jillian Rhodes appeared, looking troubled, a beautiful vase of autumn-hued flowers in her hand. Elegantly coiffed and dressed as always, she shifted her gaze to each of them in turn. "I'm here to tell you all how sorry I am."

Mara raised her eyebrows, clearly surprised by the apology from Barbara Fairmont's bosom buddy.

But Adam supposed the principal might be rethinking that relationship, considering Babzilla's arrest for disorderly conduct and public intoxication after he'd spoken to the sheriff last night. Adam wondered how Red Bluff's cruelest gossip was enjoying being the subject of the latest rumors.

Looking to Rebecca, Jillian Rhodes said, "It was wrong of me to say you had to change classes. A terrible mistake. Do you understand that?"

Clearly nervous, Rebecca looked first at her father and then at Mara before asking, "Does this mean I can go back to school?"

"Of course I want you back, Rebecca." Mrs. Rhodes set the vase atop the rolling table.

"We've made other arrangements," Adam said stiffly, still furious over the way the principal had hurt both his daughter and Mara.

"I understand you're still upset with me," Mrs. Rhodes

said. "And you have every right to be. I thought I was doing the right thing, but…I've been given to understand I may have reacted a bit hastily. I apologize for that."

The stiffness in her voice made him wonder whether the superintendent had given her a hard time for Rebecca being pulled from the school. Had the man forced her to come here and try to make things right?

Mara shook her head. "You weren't the only one at fault. If I'd been completely honest with you—"

Mrs. Rhodes' expression softened. "Perhaps you might have been, had I been a bit more willing to hear you out."

"Everybody makes mistakes sometimes," Rebecca piped up, looking at Adam.

Remembering, as he did, he thought, how often he had told her that on days when her mother was distracted or unhappy.

Mrs. Rhodes smiled and smoothed the girl's blond-streaked hair from her forehead. "Right, Rebecca. And one of mine was failing to do my homework."

Rebecca gaped, clearly astonished.

"So many parents complained to me about your leaving that I finally got around to reading the research that you sent me," the principal admitted to Mara. "I'll confess, it was all quite exciting. Very promising. And then I got to thinking, perhaps you really *are* the kind of teacher we need: dedicated, caring, even willing to take risks for the welfare of your students."

Adam smiled to see Mara blush.

"Come back to school, Mara," Mrs. Rhodes continued. "Please."

Mara lifted her chin. "And I could teach Rebecca?"

"It might be a bit awkward—" It was Mrs. Rhodes' turn to flush this time "—to have you seeing one of your students' parents. And certainly, living at the Jakes home—"

"Her living there will be perfectly natural." Adam looked into Mara's beautiful face and thought of all they'd been through, all the two of them had suffered to find each other once again. He wasn't about to let it be for nothing—wasn't about to allow the hand he'd clasped so fervently to slip out of his grasp.

Dropping to his knees, he took that hand and kissed it. "Marry me, Mara. Marry me and make me the happiest man alive."

Her green eyes filled, and in the silence that followed, he heard what sounded like a whispered prayer from Rebecca.

"Please say yes, please say yes, please say yes...."

"Yes, yes, *yes*," Mara said, laughing, and pulled him into the first kiss of their future, the kiss that marked the start of an extraordinary new adventure: a marriage with the very first woman who had ever loved him, the pesky little girl with scabby knees and ugly glasses who had grown up to become the living key to all his dreams.

* * * * *

A sneaky peek at next month...

INTRIGUE...

BREATHTAKING ROMANTIC SUSPENSE

My wish list for next month's titles...

In stores from 16th September 2011:

❏ Indestructible – Cassie Miles

❏ Enigma – Carla Cassidy

❏ Christmas Countdown – Jan Hambright

❏ Night Moves – HelenKay Dimon

❏ No Ordinary Hero – Rachel Lee

❏ Operation: Forbidden – Lindsay McKenna

❏ Boots and Bullets – BJ Daniels

Available at WHSmith, Tesco, Asda, Eason, Amazon and Apple

Just can't wait?